THE LADY

D1562447

THE

LADY

BY

CONRAD RICHTER

University of Nebraska Press
Lincoln and London

First Bison Book printing: March 1984
Most recent printing indicated by the first digit below:
1   2   3   4   5   6   7   8   9   10

Library of Congress Cataloging in Publication Data
Richter, Conrad, 1890–1968.
  The lady.
  Reprint. Originally published: New York : Knopf, c1957.
  I. Title.
PS3535.I429L3 1984   813'.52   84-20808
ISBN 0-8032-8918-9 (pbk.)

Reprinted by arrangement with Alfred A. Knopf, Inc.

To Erd

ACKNOWLEDGMENTS

THE AUTHOR acknowledges his debt to Mrs. Lou Hardy Hittson and Mrs. Cora Cosand for their memories of the old West; to Judge C. M. Botts, who kindly read and criticized the manuscript; to Ehrman B. Mitchell and John Jones, who furnished material; to John Callender, Esq., who gave counsel; to Mrs. Ruth Laughlin Alexander, Dr. Harry R. Warfel, and Judge H. H. McDonald, who made suggestions; and to many others, friends and acquaintances, who during the author's years in New Mexico recounted to him their observations and recollections of life in the beloved territory.

THE LADY

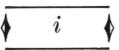

I WOULD never believe that my father had run away with the money.

Oh, I knew well enough what the people of Moro were saying: that no one really knew anything about us but Judge Sessions and he had known only my mother; that my father was too fancy a dresser to be an honest "commission boy"; that he used to pay attention to a questionable woman, Mrs. Consuelo Blount, who less than a month before had left the country, and that they were probably together somewhere in Colorado right now.

It was a barefaced lie, I told anyone who spoke it in my hearing. I said he had gone to Mrs. Blount only to learn Spanish, which he needed at the commission house. I said many other things to his credit, and not a word of the two bad things I knew he had really done, one of them being with another woman while my mother lay in her last illness back in Missouri, and the other, his unwillingness to bring her West when they found she had lung fever. She had wanted to come. The malady ran in the family. Her cousin Albert had been expected to die with it, but he had gone to New Mexico territory, where he studied law, had married into a wealthy Spanish family, and was now a judge for three or four counties, riding or driving the circuit as well as anybody.

I can still hear my mother tell my father that if she got away from the steamy air of the Missouri, she believed she would be well and could be up and get his meals again. But he had breathed the air of the Missouri all his life, he told her, and it hadn't hurt him. Only after her death did he quit the other woman, give up the house, and hunt up my mother's cousin in New Mexico, which was as far as the railroad ran then. He said he did it for me, to save me from the weak lungs of my family, but I rather thought it remorse. He wanted to get a little virtue from doing at last the thing he had so bitterly failed to do before.

However, many men fail their wives without failing their employers. My father wasn't the sort to do both. I have his photograph now, on the thick shiny brown cardboard they used then, with a zigzag curlycue for a line at the bottom, the whole thing yellow with age. It's hard to believe that he was only twenty-nine years old. He looks forty, a fine figure of a man with a soft brown mustache and white hands which in Missouri never did much more than toil on the white pages of ledgers. He carried himself straight in his well-cut clothes, and his eyes looked out at you steadily. Never, I felt, would he have abandoned me in a place like Moro, a thousand miles from Missouri, and if some woman could have made him do such a thing, as they say women can, it wasn't in him to have gone off with so little fuss, as if he'd be seeing me the next day or the one after that and knowing all the time that he was deserting me for good. He didn't even raise the whip or look back as he drove off in one of the rigs from Caldwell's Livery Stable. I followed him on foot over the acequia madre to the Quintana ranch lane and stood by one of the adobe gateposts watching his dust till buckboard and white-footed bay horse were lost in the blurred horizon.

Only one thing troubled me, and I tried not to think of it. Why hadn't he let me go along? He was driving, he said, to the vicinity of the Greenhorn Mountains, which the Mexicans call La Sierra, a range that reaches its back two and a half miles into the blue sky. Most of the year it's topped with snow. I was crazy to go with him and had begged him to take me. He had the room and packed nothing more than a sack or two of oats that I could see. But he said, no, he couldn't and wouldn't tell why.

Later on we knew that old Boreas Luna had sent two of his Mexicans down to the commission house for cash to buy another flock of sheep, that Mr. Kidd hadn't trusted the money to them, and so had sent it special with my father, in gold eagles and a few silver dollars, all done up in tight rolls of newspaper wrapped in sacking, sewed compactly, and hidden at the bottom of the oats. There were different accounts of the amount going around. Some said six thousand and some swore it was eleven, but all agreed it was what the commission house owed old Boreas for his wool clip, less what stood against his name on the company books.

About every day after that I went down to see if my father had come back. It was a long walk and no shade after leaving the cottonwoods of Old Town. Except for the several blocks of business district

near the depot, the buildings of New Town were
spread over a large area of desert, where they stood
exposed to the brassy New Mexican sun. Two years
before this when the railroad had come to the territory, everybody thought it would run through Old
Town. But the railroad people were too smart for
that. They weren't building the railroad to develop
the country, Mr. Younger at the commission house
said, but to make money. The land at Old Town was
watered by acequias and owned by old Mexican
families who would have profited. So the engineers
ran the railroad where they could get land for little
or nothing. They set the station right out on the
desert and tacked the sign MORO on it. This was
going to be the town now, they said, and they sold
plots of cheap desert land at fancy prices.

On my way I passed Caldwell's Livery Stable. It
wasn't much of a stable then, just a low adobe
building big enough for an office and bunk room
pegged around the walls for harness. Most of the
rigs were kept outside and the horses in a corral,
where they stood listless in the heat of summer and
snow of winter. A long way off I could see that the
bay with white feet wasn't there. That didn't prove
anything, I told myself stoutly. My father and his
horse might both be down at the commission house.

The sign on the commission house read: KIDD &

Co., *Forwarding and Commission Merchants.* The buildings stood by the railroad track so freight cars could load and unload in the huge man-made caves. The largest held the offices, among other things, and the first thing I looked for was my father's desk with the rickety pine case of pigeonholes above it, the top ones much higher than I could reach. As a rule, ledgers and daybooks lay open together with bills and bills of lading, all held down by lumps-of-ore paperweights, and the pigeonholes were stuffed with yellow sheets. But now pigeonholes, desk, and stool all had a bare emptiness that gave me suddenly a sick feeling. Men were coming and going, but none of them turned out to be the one I hoped to see, and I went on to where I used to find him sometimes, in the dark warehouse aisles smelling of tea and green coffee, of dyes from the bales of ginghams and calicos, of rope and saddles, of boots and sides of leather, of bacon and lard, of the cold metallic smell of hardware, the good sharp scent of tobacco, and the strong chemical odor of sheep-dip.

He wasn't there, nor on the great splintery platforms where freight wagons and pack trains were loaded, so I went to the feed warehouse, which I liked best. Here were walls of flour piled in sacks and barrels, and bins of corn, barley and oats and chop, the latter of which always smelled good enough to eat. Only the feedhouse men were there, and I went on to the last of the warehouses and the only ill-smelling one. More than once had I seen it piled to the roof with rotting hides and greasy fleeces. It was the custom then to send the latter out to the scouring mills, of which Moro had three, and when the wool came back it was light and fluffy. Often had I jumped into the huge bins and rolled around in the soft drifts, but today I only looked into the dark hot cavern and then went back to the office to try to find out when my father was coming.

The men had always been very friendly. Now they hardly let on that I was there. Only Mr. Kidd would actually look at me. He was a thick, bald-headed man with black mustache and eyebrows, and when he caught sight of me his dark eyes would flash and he'd bark low and short to one of the men. This man would speak to Mr. Younger. Neither would look my way, but I knew it was about me they had spoken. After a while Mr. Younger would come over to me.

He was a small man like Mr. Kidd but slight and wiry. I learned there that you could never go on names, because Mr. Kidd was old and Mr. Younger even older.

"How are you today, Jud?" he'd say, and his hard-bitten face would give me a smile.

"Is he back?" I'd ask, quick hope from his cheerfulness rising in me.

At that Mr. Younger's eyes would turn a bleak blue while his face kept on smiling.

"Not yet. At least not so far as I know," he'd say as if to make my father's absence less final and to hold out a hope of him still coming, although all of them knew then that old Boreas had sent word he had seen neither the money nor my father.

I'd stand for a little while, digesting the disappointment and getting hold of myself.

"Could you use a boy today?" I'd ask him.

"Not right today," he'd say thoughtfully and no hint that they wouldn't hire or trust the son of a man who ran off with eleven thousand dollars, just regret that there was no opening, and the door left open for tomorrow.

So I'd hang around another minute trying to think of something else to say, but the mind of a boy doesn't work very well under circumstances like that, and the sixty seconds of a minute are mighty long when you've transacted your business, shot your bolt for the day, and you knew they were waiting for you to go. After all, there was another day. My father might come home tomorrow or even tonight. The commission house never closed. Day

and night it was open to freighters, who kept arriving at all hours.

I don't know how long this might have gone on
if one morning I hadn't come in and found a new
man working at my father's desk. The sight of
someone there sent my hopes soaring at first, but
when I saw it was not my father, it shook me. I
knew then, despite what Mr. Younger implied, they
never expected to see my father back, and for a
long time I didn't go in again.

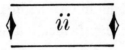

ii

My FATHER and I had rooms in what had once been a fine house on the plaza. People still called it La Casa Nuñoz after the original owner although the adobe was badly washed and all the rooms facing the street had become shops and a Mexican restaurant. Like most native buildings, it had but one story. To the rear and facing the south was a large patio like a hotel courtyard with a gallery running partway around it. There were in the patio: a well, a massive cottonwood, and by day a swarm of chil-

dren, together with a parrot in a woven willow cage.
The parrot belonged to the Padillas.

We weren't burdened with furniture, just a hard
Mexican bed, a chair, and my father's brassbound
trunk in one room; a wood cookstove, pine table,
chair, small bench, a few dishes, and water bucket
in the other. Most times we dined here on eggs
from local ranchers and on bacon, crackers, coffee,
dried fruit, and pickles my father got wholesale at
the commission house. The smells of La Sena drifted
constantly in our rooms, but we never ate there. On
special occasions my father took me to the Railroad House in the new town.

At first when my father didn't return, I lay
awake half the night wondering what would become
of me. Hailing from Missouri, my father thought
himself superior to the Mexicans and sometimes
had embarrassed me by showing it in front of them.
Lying there in bed, I could imagine them talking
among themselves with satisfaction of the just fate
that had befallen the Anglo boy whose father had
run off with Señor Kidd's gold.

How little I knew of Mexicans then, of their natural sympathies and pity for someone whose father
or brother had come afoul the law! I found that instead of hating me, the native women and girls gave
me soft pitying or bright admiring glances from

their dark eyes as I passed. Both Señora Padilla and Señora José García fed me tortillas. But it was another of Spanish blood who was my deliverer and ministering angel.

This was the lady called Doña Ellen, the wife of my mother's cousin, Albert Sessions. A native-born New Mexican, she was the daughter of a Mexican mother and English father. Of course, I knew that New Mexico was a territory of the United States and its natives were citizens of our country, and yet to me it was as if Cousin Albert had married some-one foreign as from Guatemala or Brazil. Cousin Albert always spoke to me on the street, but his wife had never recognized or spoken to me, perhaps be-cause I so assiduously avoided her.

This very day I had seen her around town in her fancy buggy with space under the sides of the seat for the rubber-tired, brass-rimmed wheels to turn with a flourish. The buggy had yellow spokes, brass lamps on either side of the patent-leather dash-board, and a matching yellow cloth top that could be thrown back as in convertible cars today. The buggy top was generally up to shield Doña Ellen from the New Mexican sun. I had just passed the lumber yard in New Town headed for home when I heard a rig overtake me and saw its wheels stop be-side me in the deep floury dust. When I looked up, there were the stylish undercut buggy with the yellow top and the lady herself holding the tan reins.

"Good afternoon, Jud. You are Jud, aren't you?" she asked brightly. "You're the very one I hoped to see. Won't you get in with me and I'll drive you back to Old Town."

To my surprise, her accent was English rather than Spanish. The stylish slant of her sailor straw and the genteel softness of her driving gloves were certainly non-Mexican, her hair, a golden Anglo color against her blue eyes. But never would I get in beside her at that moment. There flashed through my mind the tale they told of her Spanish temper and her wild English love for horses. They said she was a girl away at convent school when a mozo had put a spade bit on her favorite riding horse and after long and cruel training taught him to bow low. When the girl came home from school, he had proudly showed her horse off to her, but one look at the maimed and bleeding mouth, and she had struck the mozo down with the heavy end of her crop. The story was that she had killed him.

When I asked my father he said he didn't know if it was true or not, but I must remember she was a Johnson y Campo, that the Johnson y Campo sheep ranch took in a great Spanish grant beyond the Prietas. For generations her people had had the power of life and death over their peons, especially here in the Arriba country, and a fine horse to them meant more than a peon.

When I held off from the buggy, I expected her to drive away with English abruptness and dismissal, but she was all feminine Mexican wile now.

"Don't you want to ride with me, Jud?" she asked, wrinkling her eyebrows at me in that playful Spanish gesture of hurt, a characteristic I was to see in her a thousand times afterward, a trick of expression almost childlike, she who was anything but a child. At the same time that she spoke to me so lightly, there was something indefinably sad about her. I suspect now it was only the faint inconsolable melancholy of her Latin blood. But at the time it seemed like something else, as if some secret past grief sucked the joy of life from her. I remembered how quick the Mexicans said she was to violent anger and complete forgiveness, and I think that is what quieted my fear and stitched a bond between us, this secret sorrow of hers like mine and her complete forgiveness of me for the crime of which my father was accused.

There was something else I didn't recognize at first, in fact not for weeks afterward, but which I learned to observe and know so well. This was her complex femininity. She could be very capable, determined, willful, also satiric and funny at times. All this on occasion could vanish and an appealing helplessness come into her blue eyes and even into the way she sat or stood, so that others, and especially men, could not forbear rescuing her, throwing themselves into her cause, bringing to pass what she wished, indeed doing it with masculine pleasure and great satisfaction to themselves.

Today she seemed to me innocent as beautiful, what she asked so reasonable, even tolerant, that before I knew it I was stumbling around the wheels and climbing up on the cushions which in most buggies were hard black leather but which here were of soft rose cloth, and we were off down the road with a feeling that no automobile can give me today, of flowing animal limbs and muscles, of a bright tan harness with silver trimmings and a silver whip socket engraved with a name in script that I couldn't read. Everyone, I noticed, looked up with lively interest to see us go by as almost no one looks at a car today. I saw with pride that she drove her favorite horse I had heard so much about, the fastest in the territory and her great pet. I remembered my father saying that when he asked her how many children she had, she had told him two, both boys, one nine and one seven years old. My father learned later that she had given birth to only one child, my cousin Willy, whom I had never met, and that by her seven-year-old boy she must have meant this horse called Critter, who had been named by her father half in jest before he died.

Presently we stopped in front of the large shabby Casa Nuñoz. Here she cut the horse to my side so she could alight.

"Will you hold him for me?" she asked. "Critter hates to be tied. If we were out on the mesa, I'd let him stand, but he's so curious. He likes to move here and there and examine everything, and I don't want him wandering around town with a buggy."

Never had I held a horse, and I felt sure this one she called Critter knew it. He was dark, not black, middle, or red bay, the latter of which the Mexicans call colorado. Rather he was a shade called oscura, which is sometimes only a dirty color but in Critter was a peculiar shade of brown. For the first time I was close enough to see faint inner black markings like on certain furs rich ladies wear. He was not stylish like they, however. There was no check rein and now that he had stopped he rather lounged. I had seen much more handsome and spirited horses and wondered why a lady like Mrs. Sessions with such a fancy buggy liked him well enough to consider him one of her boys.

Today I was to get an inkling of the reason. As

I took his bridle I saw him examine me quietly, almost benignly, from the great round world of his eye, in which I could make out a curious image of myself and of the Casa Nuñoz behind me. He saw my fear of him, I'm sure. I also like to think that he saw the confused loneliness of an insecure and half-starved boy. This may be pure imagination on my part. Be that as it may, after a minute or two I was no longer afraid but absorbed in watching him. He had apparently accepted me and turned his attention to his surroundings. I could have sworn that he surveyed intelligently and in turn the church, the bell towers, the Sisters' school next to it, the bandstand in the center of the little park, and La Casa Nuñoz closer at hand. From time to time he would turn his attention to things that passed, horses, riders, vehicles, drivers, foot travelers, children, and even a yellow butterfly. His ears constantly worked back and forward like pointers of mental acquisitiveness. I had the curious feeling that he observed and speculated on the large goiter of Mrs. Montoya as she crossed the plaza and the purpose of Xavier Sandoval and his carpenters as they trimmed and planed several new vigas for the church under the great cottonwood that stood over the entrance.

Mrs. Sessions stayed in the house a long time. I

saw young Gus Padilla run out and come back with old Ezequiel Salazar, the owner of Casa Nuñoz. Then the boy reappeared and with importance took hold of Critter's bridle.

"Doña Ellen wants to see you inside," he informed me.

I went, somewhat puzzled and reluctant. In my father's and my rooms I found a little group of people including old Ezequiel, Mrs. García, Mrs. Padilla, and a number of their children, all at a respectful distance from Mrs. Sessions, who in some unexplained way made our kitchen seem rude and barbarous, unfit to hold such a lady as she.

"Jud, we've been holding a little junta about you," she said almost gaily.

I stood startled and awkward, not knowing what to make of it, but convinced that whatever the purpose it was not good. Mrs. Sessions went on.

"The judge and I don't like you living here by yourself. It's not well for a young boy and we're afraid you don't get enough to eat. How would you like to come over to my house and stay till your father gets back?"

"I don't think I would like it," I said quickly.

"He would like it fine, Doña Ellen," Mrs. García informed in Spanish, and old Ezequiel added solemnly that what I said should be considered as from an ignorant boy who didn't know what he was saying, that in truth I would be overjoyed to live there.

"No, I want to stay here!" I stammered, retreating toward the door, but the stout form of Mrs. Padilla blocked my way.

"He is in reality very unhappy and lonely here, Doña Ellen," she declared.

"How can he expect to live here alone?" that old villain Ezequiel added. "Since his father left him, he never sent him a peso to pay for these rooms. To make ends meet I should rent them to Abundio Sais, who asked me about them."

"It isn't good for him to be so much alone, Doña," Mrs. García spoke up. "In your house he would have Epifania and Manuel for company now, and later on when you came to town he would have your son. It is no small thing to have a cousin to play with and speak with and read and spell the English language with."

"I'm a bad reader and speller," I protested.

Old Ezequiel waved his hand.

"You mustn't be deceived by his tricks, Doña Ellen. His father could read and write very well or never could he have been a trusted clerk and messenger of the commission house. Like father, like son," he added, after which his black eyes gazed triumphantly at me as if he had given me the black name I deserved for opposing my eviction from the premises.

"That's enough!" Cousin Albert's wife reproved sharply, and I thought I saw her eyes blaze at him for a moment. Then to me as if it was all decided: "Manuel will come for your trunk and other things. Now let's go over to the house and I'll show you where you will sleep."

She took my arm. I felt the strong pressure of her hand and that there was no further use to try to escape or rebel. Before I knew it we were out on the plaza, where she left Critter looking curiously after her while we went on foot near by to a street called La Placita, one of the spokes radiating from the square.

The white Sessions house, known as the Johnson y Campo house, looked large and imposing to me. The front door was locked, but Cousin Albert's wife didn't give up and go around to another door. She pulled the fancy bellrope and stood her ground till it was opened by a flurried Mexican woman whom she called Epifania. Doña Ellen waited. I expected a scene, at least a reprimand from the Spanish temper, but there was just a silent moment between them. Then we entered.

I found myself in an immense dim hall, wide as a

parlor and twice as long, with mysterious doors on either side, one of which was open, revealing ghostly shapes of sheets over indeterminate pieces of furniture. Mrs. Sessions showed me that new and astonishing institution she called the bathroom, a frightening place with a great white tin tub on a high platform as if on a throne, after which she took me to a much nicer room with a white iron bed, the figure of Christ on the cross on a wall, and soft washed Navajo rugs on the floor. This was Willy's room, she told me, and would be mine until they moved in, when another bed would be put in for me.

"You are all right now, Jud," she promised me. "Friends of your father will look after you till he gets back."

Her references to my father and his friends, and that he would be back, warmed me like wine and bathed all the strange objects around me. But after she had gone something went out of the house. It seemed foreign. Even its air smelled like incense. Unseen presences with a strong Spanish will and flavor seemed to come out of hiding to cast their influence in the air, presences much more native and alien than Cousin Albert's wife and, I felt, not so favorably disposed toward me.

After going to bed I remembered what my father had said of the Johnson y Campo family, its power

over life and death of its peons, and the story of
Doña Ellen and the mozo who had incurred her dis-
pleasure. The act, they said, had occurred more
than ten years ago some twenty miles distant on
the other side of the Prietas, and yet I could imagine the poor Mexican struck down and lying
senseless outside my window. There came to me the
peculiar memory of the lady's hands today as they
had held the reins and as one of them had taken my
arm. Once later on I heard her say amusedly that
her hands didn't match the rest of her, that they
were too large, that driving and especially holding
back fast horses from her youth had developed
them abnormally. I could see nothing large about
them. All I felt tonight was a certain indefinable
power and mastery in them. I was glad that she
and Cousin Albert planned to stay out on the ranch
until fall. By that time, I was sure that my father
would be back.

NEXT MORNING with the New Mexican sun shining in my window and lying brightly across the kitchen floor during breakfast, the house seemed like a different place, and the world, too. Not only then but after I sallied forth from the house, I found my status in Old Town had changed.

Old Ezequiel, with drooping eye, crooked stick, and the picture of avarice and chicanery, stopped me on the plaza to talk to me with deference in front of everyone. Lawyer Beasley, whose house stood next door to my Cousin Albert's—they had married sisters—acknowledged my existence by inclining his head curtly but unmistakably to me when he passed. And the Old Town boys talked to me of my absent father with new and evident respect.

"Your papa will be back soon now," Goyo Sánchez, whose full name was Gregorio, promised me. "His cousin the judge will see that he goes free."

"For a while he may go to jail, but it will not be so bad," Pas Ramírez assured. "My Uncle Ángel is in the penitentiary at Santa Fe for six years. They let him come home for weddings and funerals."

"Yes, and you'll have Señor Kidd's eleven thousand pesos besides"—this from Lino García, whose full name was Rosalino. He was financially minded, delivering barrels of water from the river to residents of New Town who had no wells as yet.

I answered angrily that my father had never taken the money, but they looked at me with instant dismay and disappointment. I saw that I was losing caste, that I must not object to my rank as embezzler's son if I wanted to swim with them in the river, rope milk cows pastured in the Big Bosque, and ride barebacked, often naked, some of the broken-down horses grazing there. At Epifania's orders, I went back to the house for midday dinner and found a great dish of frijoles, hot with chile that burned all the way down. When she asked how I liked them I could only say "Muy bueno" with tears running down my cheeks. Epifania thought I cried because of my hunger and her kindness in supplying it. She kept filling my plate. I couldn't stop her, and all the way back to the Big Bosque my insides were on fire.

But it was the first day my stomach had been filled since my father left, and late that afternoon coming back for supper, with the late sun slanting through the cottonwoods and time standing still as it does in New Mexico, with the stillness unbroken save for the drawn-out call of the mourning dove, I felt that life was sweet again, and the one who had saved me was Cousin Albert's lady, who had put me under her ægis and the protection of the powerful Johnson y Campo name. As I turned up La Placita from the plaza, the walls of her and Cousin Albert's house ahead of me glistened white in the sun like a citadel of peace and security which could not easily be broken.

In this I found that I was mistaken.

My first inkling came the second week the judge moved back to town. He had come alone at first, called by the September term of court. He slept in the Old Town house during the week, returning to

the ranch for the weekend. Any uneasiness I felt
for his coming soon vanished. He had me call him
Cousin Albert like my mother used to do, and
treated me kindly, almost as a son, a slender delicate man with a white skin and unusual heavy
black beard. This together with his deep voice and
powerful phrases never ceased to surprise me in
one so frail. Sheets still hung over the furniture in
the parlor, and tonight as usual he sat in the wide
hall by the hanging brass lamp which he had pulled
down to read the Denver paper that had come on
the evening train. In the shadows on a settee, I lay
content just to be near this one remaining link to
my mother. Presently the hand bell on the end of
the long cord that ran to the rear of the house
tinkled, and the judge rose with the paper still in
his hands and went to the door himself.

"Oh, good evening, Amado. Come in," he said
heartily, and I saw a durably dressed Mexican with
strong, brown, almost Oriental face and eyes. I knew
him as Sheriff Martínez. There were two Martínez
brothers in Moro. It was the custom for Amado to
run for sheriff on the Republican ticket and Fran-
cisco on the Democratic. Whichever won appointed
his brother as first deputy, and a Martínez had
been sheriff for Moro County since most men could
remember. Usually it was Amado. At his silence to-

night and the grave way he entered, I saw Cousin
Albert's heartiness dissipate.

"Is anything the matter?" he asked.

"You haven't heard from the ranch?"

"You mean our ranch?" Cousin Albert seemed
surprised. "Sit down, Amado."

But both men remained standing.

"You remember last year, Judge, when Señor
Beasley drove his herd through Ojo Canyon? I
don't mean that Señor Beasley was there himself.
But his foreman said his patrón told him it was too
far to drive around on the public road through
Canyon del Norte. The cattle would lose weight. His
patrón said his wife was a Johnson y Campo herself, a sister of Doña Ellen, and that Jeffcoat could
come through. Riders and buckboards came through
all the time and they were never stopped. Now Señor
Beasley knows very well how narrow Ojo Canyon is.
I didn't see for myself what the cattle did to your
señora's garden, but I heard. Also what Doña Ellen
thought of that garden. Your señora and Jeffcoat
had very hard words. She warned him never to come
over your private road with a herd again."

"Yes, yes, of course," the judge said impatiently
as if to urge him on.

"Well, Jeffcoat's men came through again this
morning. He had a herd of fat steers Señor Beasley

wanted to ship before the early price dropped. So he took Ojo Canyon like the other time. There was Doña Ellen's new garden and rosebushes and a new fence around them. Jeffcoat did not stop."

"We mustn't blame Jeffcoat. This is Beasley's doings," Cousin Albert said angrily.

"Perhaps," the sheriff spoke under his breath with dry Spanish malice, "perhaps it is a pity that Señor Beasley wasn't there instead of Jeffcoat."

The judge looked sober. "You mean someone was hurt."

"About as bad as a man can be hurt," the sheriff said gravely. "From all reports, there was only one shot. I saw for myself that it was a very good shot. The bullet found the forehead."

The judge stood almost like a statue.

"Did his men say who did it?"

The sheriff avoided his eyes. "Who knows? A herd of cattle makes much dust. It is hard to see. But all could hear the rifle speak. It came, they said, from the portal of your house."

"How long was the shot?"

"From all accounts," the sheriff repeated, looking away, "it was a long shot and a very good one."

Cousin Albert was silent for a while as if wrestling with something grave.

"Well, I expect you to do whatever is right and necessary, Amado."

"Gracias á Dios, I don't have to do anything. Don Carlos came in tonight. He said it was him who fired the shot."

"Charley! Why didn't he come here to see me?"

"He told me he thought you wouldn't like to leave him out on bail on a murder charge. So I left him with Choppo and came right over."

"Thank you, Amado." I could see that Cousin Albert was much affected. He folded his paper and laid it on the table. Then he took his large cream-colored hat from the rack.

"I'll walk along back with you and talk to him," he said. "Meantime, you better send for Tom."

For a long time after they had gone, and later in my bed, I lay going over what was said and the pictures created in my mind. There had been something incomplete about the story, something that passed between the two men that puzzled me, something not so much spoken as left unsaid but which each understood. I wondered how Charley could have done such a violent thing. They said that he had once been a good enough shot with the rifle, trained by his English father, but of late the only things he was known to do were drink whisky and drive fast horses.

He was still more blond than Doña Ellen. We boys called him the Englishman, not only from his light hair and florid cheeks but because of his eccentricities and curious British nature. He was one of the reasons we went to New Town on Saturday evenings. Then the Englishman could be found in town drinking at the Antlers Bar. Punctually at eight o'clock he would come out, unknot the hitching-rope, get in his buggy, and race his fast horse up and down the two blocks of business street. On the way back he was invariably halted and fined for exceeding the speed limit. With evident satisfaction he would pay the fine and go back to the bar, while the spectators collected for the event would reluctantly scatter.

Next morning when I got up Cousin Albert was already gone, but Pas and Goyo were waiting for me outside the back door. They informed me that the Englishman's horse was in our stable, and we spent the greater part of the morning standing around him talking in suppressed excitement. It was the same bahío with black mane and tail we had seen the Englishman race last Saturday night. It gave me a curious feeling to see him standing there so calmly, shoving his nose into the hay and energetically chewing, unaware that his master was locked up for murder only a few blocks away.

"It is his horse," Pas said at length. "But it is
not he, they say, that killed the Anglo."

"Who was he, then?" I asked, eager to hear the
family name cleared.

"It was not a he, but a she," Pas declared mys-
teriously.

For a moment I didn't know what he meant. Then
I saw Manuel bearing down upon us. Doña Ellen
always referred to him as a mozo, which meant
"boy," but he was some fifty years old, a short
heavy man like so many Mexicans his age, with a
powerful torso and tremendous face now distorted
with rage.

"What lie is this, you son-of-a-goat!" he roared
and tried to get his huge hands on Pas. Those
hands, it was said, could rope the wildest running
horse in a corral and bring him to a stop without
snubbing-post or saddle horn. If they had got hold
of Pas, there was no telling what they might have
done, but Pas was too quick for him and dodged out
in the alley, where we presently joined him.

"Now let's go down to the jail," Pas said dar-
ingly. "We will ask the Englishman himself who
fired the shot that killed Señor Jeffcoat."

All the way down the alley what he had said
earlier pierced me. Exactly what did he mean that
it had not been a he but a she that had done it? It

came back to plague me now that Sheriff Martínez
had not used the word "man" as the expert with
the rifle who had fired the shot, but "person." I remembered the story about Doña Ellen as a girl. A
whole procession of uneasy thoughts troubled me
as we stood outside the jail under a small window
which Pas and Goyo informed me opened into the
Englishman's cell. Although Pas called loudly and
brazenly, no face appeared at the bars and no voice
answered.

It was late noon when I came back up the alley
to find Doña Ellen's buggy outside the stable and
her pet horse, Critter, in the next box stall to her
brother's bahío. An empty carriage that had evidently been filled with baggage and criadas from
the ranch stood in the driveway while its horses out
in the alley chewed corn from nose bags before start-
ing back to the Prietas.

Manuel scowled at me.

"You better make steps for the house. If you are
wise you will say nothing from that young liar of a
he goat," he warned me.

The rite of dinner at such a time I would have
gladly avoided, but Manuel herded me ahead of him
toward the back door with all the energy of a
loader who slaps his thighs and cries "Hu-cha!"

while driving sheep onto the cattle cars. Not wishing to be a sheep, I ran around to the front door.

The house seemed another place when I entered it. Moving slowly down the hall, I saw that the sheets had been taken from the familiar shapes in the long parlor, disclosing wholly unfamiliar furnishings. There were twin scarlet sofas with rolled ends, chairs in red-and-gold brocade that looked like Mexico, a tall object with filigree brass legs rising to marble shelves and crowned with a painted china lamp. Broad walnut frames inlaid with gold on the wall held only the tiniest of pictures. Another frame enclosed a wreath and one a bunch of withered flowers, mementos of some funeral.

The doors to the other rooms opening on the wide hall were open now and I saw across the way a second parlor, not so long as the other, but with a couch, an organ, a blue fireplace, a globe on a stand, and a lacy nest of artificial flowers hanging from the ceiling. As I went on I had glimpses into other high-ceiling rooms, furnished with heavy and ornate brass beds, canopies, marble-top bureaus, dressers, and tables, engravings on the walls, china lamps in various sizes, Brussels carpet on the floor. Most every room had in addition to the bed a couch or lounge of some kind. I had never seen such a lot of them in a single house. A stranger would suppose the Johnson y Campos the laziest and sleepiest of families.

I stopped before reaching the dining-room, but Doña Ellen must have seen my head pass outside the window, else she heard the front door. She came out in the hall looking even more delicate and blue-eyed than I remembered.

"Hello, Jud! Where have you been?" she greeted, as if I and not she was the one who needed comforting. "We've had to start. Come in."

She took my cold hand in her warm one and drew me into the dining-room, where dinner stood on the massive table affixed to the floor, flanked by long polished benches of enormous pine planking on either side.

"This is Willy," she said, leading me where a dark-haired, delicate-looking boy sat in front of a scarcely touched plate. "Your place, Jud, is right beside him. I hope you two will be friends. You're cousins, you know, and blood is thicker than water."

Once I was settled long enough to recover myself and observe what was going on around me, I saw Cousin Albert at the head of the table looking kindly and approvingly at me. His wife didn't take her seat where I expected, but sat opposite Willy and me. I soon found that she needed no formal position at the doña's head of the table to hold court, but could take care of herself wherever she was.

Before I came she had evidently been telling the judge and Willy of some incident. Now I listened to her, a little surprised to find it amusing. She finished, turned to me, asked me questions about myself, confided to me one or two intimate things about the ranch, then wove the four of us into her conversation. Her flow of talk was fluent, Spanish in character but spoken in English for my benefit and managed with both English and Spanish skill. It was impossible not to listen and watch, too. She seemed to make light of their unspoken affliction.

I found this a characteristic I was to see much of, her manner of disregarding trouble and danger by making fun of them both. It was this, I think, together with her playful feminine wile and Latin melancholy, as if deep inside of her she knew her serious fate all the time, that made men want to deliver her from the dangers she so confidently disdained and the trouble she so rashly courted.

At first, sitting there at the table, I wondered if shooting and death had actually occurred. Then with dinner done, it was as if the pleasant interlude, like an act in a play, was over. Faint sadness settled on her face. Gravity returned to Cousin Albert. When I glanced at Willy his dark eyes looked

back at me wordlessly. What the look meant I had
no idea, but I felt that I liked him and that we would
get along.

There was no telephone in the house those days
to inform your friends that you had come to town,
but news traveled about as fast then as now, par-
ticularly upon an event like this when your friends
were expected to rally around and offer support and
encouragement. It was something of a revelation to
see the house bright and almost gay that evening,
with wine in glasses taken from a rack of four
marble shelves along the wall. The Ignacio Bacas
and the Felipe Chávezes, who spoke mostly Spanish,
came, and the Wilmots and the Kidds, who spoke
mostly English. These were sheep people or those
who did business with them.

Others arriving later included Tom Dold, the
family lawyer since Cousin Albert had sat on the
bench. A bachelor like Mr. Younger, he reminded
me of him also in his fund of good humor, but was
portlier, had a more courteous gentlemanly air and
slower Alabama or Mississippi speech. Not a word
so far that I heard in English was spoken of Ellen's
brother languishing in jail, but Mr. Dold's stories
and confident manner spoke continuously saying,
have no fear, everything in Moro County is under
control.

When Willy and I were sent to bed, his mother
excused herself from the company and came back
to see that he was properly covered in his new quar-
ters. Late September nights can be cool in Moro.
He occupied my late bed which had been his, and
I was in another narrower one placed in the room
since last night. His mother tucked him in and
kissed him good-night. Then she came over and did
the same to me.

No one had kissed me since my mother had done
it several years before. I remembered Cousin Albert's wife's hands as brisk and masterful, but when
she pressed the covers around my neck and shoulders I thought I had never felt a touch more gentle
and soft. That such hands could have the stain of
blood on them seemed to me unthinkable. I felt myself relax, grateful that for tonight at least sleep
would solve all problems, including that of making
any more talk to Willy this first night of our ac-
quaintance when tragedy and constraint lay so
heavy on us both.

"Buenas noches, Jud," she said, using the Spanish to me as she had to Willy, as if to intimate that
I would have to learn more of the language now.

"Good night, Doña Ellen," I said.

"Call me Cousin Ellen," she corrected, and
waited.

"Good night, Cousin Ellen," I replied dutifully. She looked down at me in warm approval, but even as she smiled I imagined I saw deep inconsolable shadows in her eyes.

iv

THE MORO COUNTY courthouse stood a little way
off the plaza at the corner of Audiencia Street and
what was then called New Town Road. Today the
building looks very old and ordinary, as if always
used for mercantile purposes. But those days I
thought it imposing, a kind of family government
house since Cousin Albert held the highest office
in it and ruled over it like a king in his rude palace.

More than once I had ventured into its dim tun-
nels and gazed on doors painted with such mysterious and important names as TREASURER, ASSESSOR.

COUNTY CLERK, COMMISSIONERS, and their Spanish equivalents. The most important and exciting doors to me were marked COURTROOM and JUDGE'S CHAMBERS. The latter I had not entered, but since they were the legal offices of Cousin Albert, the door had given me a warm and proud feeling.

Now, after what had happened on the ranch, the aspect of the whole building changed. I found myself avoiding it whenever possible. Something dark, unfriendly, almost frightening had come over it and the jail where Ellen's brother, Charley, awaited trial. I knew it couldn't be Charley or his fate. He meant little or nothing to me. No, it must be something else. I remembered what Pas had hinted at. That must be the secret of my shock, an implication so incredible and terrible that I didn't dare think of it openly.

From the beginning I looked to see if anyone else might know and feel as I did. Willy came under my scrutiny first. He was a quiet boy with pale skin and a shock of heavy black Mexican hair. Although his face could light up like the sun coming out on a patch of sunflowers, there were times when he looked at me with something inexpressible in his dark eyes. I watched Cousin Albert, too, but his grave face and eyes, his gallant black beard and slender arched back told me nothing.

I waited for Willy's grandmother to come in from the ranch for the trial. They called her Mama Grande instead of the usual Abuelita. She would know, I felt, for she had been there when it happened. If she hadn't seen it herself, she surely would have demanded every detail from those who did. A short, stout native woman with a swarthy face, she had the blackest of eyes. Those eyes gave the impression of having looked on many unpleasant things, the butchery of sheep, torture by Indians, the stabbing and shooting-down of men in cold blood, and other wickedness common in this raw land. She had a tongue that ran on rapidly in Spanish like many of her kind, but her face and black eyes to me remained unreadable.

When Ellen's sister, Doña Ana, came over from next door to see her mother, I thought I caught a glimpse of fear in her face, but I felt it might have been for her husband. Even before coming to my cousin's house to live I had heard how since their marriage Lawyer Beasley had dominated and restrained her, taking over her inheritance, keeping her on a strict allowance, laying down her expenses for the house, naming the prices she must pay even for such small things as eggs and chile, trimming the wages of the native servants until she had to put up with some of the poorest.

Epifania had once told me how Doña Ana had looked as a girl.

"Ah, you should see those two girls together when they are little. About the same size. Only a year or more between them. But such a difference! Doña Ana morena. How you say in English?— dark. Not ugly dark. We Mexicans think dark very pretty. Dark skin, black hair, black eyes, and lively as a kitten. And Doña Ellen with white skin and hair of gold like her father. You wouldn't believe they come from the same mother."

Now I found Doña Ana older-looking than Ellen, worn-faced and somber-eyed. It was strange to see her and think that before her marriage she had been beautiful and gay. Today she seemed apprehensive, to have no will or decision of her own.

"Snell thinks I should," several times she defended herself. "I'll see what Snell thinks," she said when Ellen urged them to dinner.

She grew visibly nervous when Ellen asked if she wouldn't sit with her and her mother at the trial.

"I'm not sure what Snell wants," was all she would say.

I suspected she was here today without his permission. More than once her daughter, Felicitas, said they had better go. Doña Ana hung on as if she feared to stay but hated more to leave, as if

since this shooting had come between them she
didn't know when she would see her mother and
sister again. From the start, Felicitas refused to sit
down. I thought her the prettiest girl I had ever
seen, a little younger than I, with an English skin,
hazel eyes, and golden hair. I felt that this was
how Ellen must have looked when she was young, but
Felicitas would have little to do with her Aunt Ellen
now, regarding her with an attitude I was sure came
from her father. Indeed she treated us all with
veiled hostile coolness, as if we had shown ourselves
the bitter enemy and persecutor of her parent. Only
on Willy once or twice when he wasn't looking did
I see her glance soften.

My eyes searched the faces of others, too—of
Tom Dold and Dr. George Gammel, who were most
often at the house, as well as the Wilmots, the
Rodeys, and the Kidds. But they told me nothing.
As for the native friends who came, their faces were
impossible for an Anglo to read.

Meanwhile the trial was approaching and Willy
and I were told we would have to attend. I suspect
it was the idea of Tom Dold, who defended Charley,
that we boys sitting with Ellen and her mother
would arouse the sympathy of the jury. The most
that it aroused in me was the belief that my unspoken fears might be brought out in our presence.

All the time that Willy and I had to sit there, with
witness after witness being questioned, with every
sentence translated by the court interpreter from
Spanish to English or the other way around, with
recesses and irksome delays, with Cousin Albert sitting watchfully on the bench, and people, including
many cattlemen from out of the county, crowding
the room to the doors and windows, I remembered
what Pas Ramírez had hinted and waited for it to
raise its ugly head in the courtroom.

The witness I disliked more than any other was
Lawyer Beasley.

"That's my Uncle Snell and he hates us," Willy
had whispered the first day. "When Grandfather
died, he wanted us to let him take over and manage
the ranch. But only Tía Ana would sign."

I remembered the first time I had seen the name.
My father had brought home a copy of the *Moro
Sentinel* and in it was his advertisement:

J. SNELL BEASLEY, attorney at law
Legal Advice and Counsel. Collections Made.
Loans Arranged. Deeds. Mortgages.
All Instruments of Writing
Promptly Attended to.

My father said he was the shrewdest and richest
lawyer in the county and told me stories to prove it.

One, I recall, was how he had collected a note for the Silverio Garcías. A Baca County cattleman owed the Garcías twenty thousand dollars. For years he refused to pay. Beasley told the Garcías he would collect it in or out of court, but his fee would be half of the amount, and the Garcías finally signed a paper promising him ten thousand dollars. Then Beasley settled the debt quickly for eleven thousand. His share was ten thousand, the Garcías' only one.

Another time, my father said, Beasley was engaged by a cattleman named Lassen to defend him for the murder of a Mexican sheepherder. There was no doubt of his acquittal among the cattlemen in Baca County, but Beasley had fixed a juror to hold out for conviction, or so everyone openly said. This hung the jury, and a new trial was ordered, when Lassen was acquitted. The first time Beasley took Lassen's cattle as his fee, the second time his ranch, and this was the ranch whose foreman, Jeffcoat, had been shot in Ojo Canyon.

And now here Lawyer Beasley was in court before me. Of all the Jeffcoat sympathizers, many of them from Baca County, he was the most dangerous to reckon with. A short thick man with a red mottled face, he sat directly behind the prosecuting attorney and often leaned forward to speak to him. When at last he was put on the stand as owner of the cattle, he let loose long blasts of answers and testimony on his wife's right to send their cattle through Ojo Canyon that, I felt, shook Charley's defense to its foundations.

But no word did he breathe of the specter that lay on my heart, and when I looked up and saw Cousin Albert sitting unaffected on the bench, the faces of the jurors as before, the procedure of the court unchanged, and other witnesses being called as if nothing had happened, I had the same feeling as the night when Cousin Albert and Sheriff Martínez had talked, as if all were playing a part.

My chief hope was from something Tom Dold had said.

"Don't worry about Charley, Ellen. Every man we let on the jury has something to do with the sheep business. Or else with somebody who does. Most of them have Spanish blood besides."

But I knew that Snell Beasley was not playing a part. I think he must have expected a hung jury, for the last day he let Doña Ana make the show of attending her brother's trial. The jury was out scarcely an hour when they came in with a verdict of not guilty. Freed now, the prisoner pushed to his mother and Ellen in the crowd. Doña Ana was so carried away by the excitement that she, too, made her way to their side.

It was a pretty scene, Charley hugged and kissed by his mother and sisters while the sheepmen stood around watching with enjoyment and approval. In her emotion, Doña Ana looked years younger, and I was struck by the contrast the two sisters made to-day, Ellen with her white English skin and golden hair, and Ana dark and glowing.

Then suddenly the red face of Lawyer Beasley appeared. The excitement seemed to go out of Ana. Her face aged visibly as her husband took her arm and they moved away.

I saw soberness and pity on many faces, but it didn't bother me. My relief was too great, not so much that Charley was freed but that court and jury had recognized no other who could have fired the shot. I went home in peace. At supper Ellen said we had stood by loyally, that already we had missed so much school it wouldn't hurt us to miss a little more and so she was taking us out for a week's holiday to the ranch. It seemed then that God was back in his heaven and all was right with the world.

There was a celebration at the house that evening, with dozens of guests, including the family of Apolonio Sena, who had testified in Charley's behalf.

Next morning Charley went back to the ranch, taking his mother with him. I think the idea was to get him away from the saloons while the cattlemen were still in town.

We made ready to leave early the same afternoon. It was a cloudless fall day, of which there are so many in the Southwest. Manuel brought Critter and the yellow-top buggy around to the front of the house. The horse, which had hardly been out of his stall during the trial, was impatient to be off. As a rule with three in the buggy the driver, who must sit on the adjoining knees of the other two, would be the lightest in weight. But it was plain that Critter would be too much for a boy today, and I had to take Willy on my lap.

"It will make you strong, holding up each other," Ellen said lightly while Critter chafed to go.

Just the way she spoke to him as she took the lines gave me complete confidence which did not waver though we turned the corner of Iglesia Street on two wheels and went down what is now Center Avenue with a cloud of dust behind us.

It was exciting to ride with her again, her light talk and fun, her feminine presence very near to me, her superb mastery of horse and the desert spaces. Pleasure in my new life swam about me. Once we had forded the river and were up on the escarpment with the broad mesa stretching before us, washing up to the Prietas like a wave foaming with dried bunch grass, I could hardly wait for the hunting that she promised us. Looking ahead, the Prietas were like a long wall of dark sand sprinkled with moss, but the sand, Willy informed me, was rock and the green moss cedars and pines where mule deer and mountain lion could be found.

Halfway across the mesa we overtook a group of horsemen, evidently cattlemen returning to Baca County from the trial. They looked around and saw us coming but did not get out of our way. Ellen had to turn Critter aside on the level mesa to pass.

"Hu-cha! Hucha!" one of them sent up the sheep-man's cry derisively after us.

"Don't look back!" Ellen cautioned us, careful, I thought, neither to increase or slacken Critter's pace, but presently the same voice yelled again. I couldn't understand what it said, but I think Ellen did because when I looked at her something in her face and shoulders had changed.

I heard hoofbeats coming after us, and that was when I learned the congenital truth about Critter, that he could never let another horse around him, and at such a time not even Ellen could hold him. Now as the hoofbeats came closer, he answered with a burst of speed that left the other quickly behind.

Ellen tried to curb him. I still retain a vivid picture of her in my mind, her gloved hands sawing on the tan lines, her slight body half lifted to its feet.

"You fool!" she cried, exasperated. "They'll think we're running away."

She could do nothing with him until sounds of pursuit behind us had ceased. Then she slowed him down and furiously turned him around. The horsemen were now a mile or two in the rear, and she drove slowly back until close to them. Here in the trail she waited for them to come.

Willy and I were silent. What he thought I had no means of knowing, but when I glanced at Ellen the transformation in her astonished me. I am much older now and experience has taught me never to be surprised at the presence of fire and flint wanting only provocation to show themselves in the softest and slightest of girls and women, especially those with a blond or red coloring. But then it was a revelation to me to see with what hard relish she faced the oncoming riders. Her feminine trusting and helpless way with men had vanished and been replaced with something else, still feminine but without pity and boding no good for anyone, herself included.

Critter stood perfectly quiet while the riders

came, as if his honor was not involved so long as he
faced them. They gave the yellow-top buggy a wide
berth, turning far aside as Ellen had before. None
of them offered to molest us or even speak to her, but
when they were by and Ellen passed them again,
they let out a series of shrill derisive Texas yells.
This time she did not stop. We drove on toward the
mountains, and nothing more was said about it, but
the incident made a strong impression on me.

If I thought Ellen a lady in town, she was still
more so out here. Over the years I always thought
her to be at her best among the natives. They
seemed to infect her with a special charm. Hardly
had we approached the scattered cluster of adobe
buildings when Johnson y Campo Mexicans surrounded the buggy. They didn't run or swarm.
They appeared to be already there to celebrate, as
if they knew we were coming and could wait for us.
Time meant nothing to them, and now this was the
moment they had all looked forward to. The men
pulled off their unwieldy hats with surprising respect and grace. The swarthy women smiled. The
black eyes of the children, who were miniature repli-
cas of their elders, shone at their patrona. Even
men who looked to me like rascals and thieves asked
with gentle courtesy of the health and well-being of
Ellen and Willy, whom they called Guillo. I was

introduced as Willy's cousin, and my well-being became instantly their consuming interest and concern.

But never for a moment could I treat them as Ellen and Willy did. There was, I soon found, a great art in it, a precise stage between superiority and warm interest which I never could attain. Other Mexican ricos I had seen in town showed no such manner. Indeed, some of them treated the poor of their own race with rude and brutal contempt, and I wondered if Ellen's secret might not have been inherited from her father. For the first time I had a glimpse of him. In the long adobe horse stables, in a place called the tackroom, among the bridles, saddles, collars, and pieces of harness on the wall were tacked up photographs of Johnson y Campo horses, often with a rider or driver. Sometimes it was Ellen or Charley but usually their father, whom I found to my surprise had been a one-armed man of presence and intensity.

Where I felt him most was in the house, in what they called the gunroom, with New Mexican grizzly skins on the floor and on the wall deer, elk, and antelope heads and a considerable rack of pistols and rifles, all interstudded with photographs, some of them framed, of Ellen's father standing with his foot on a prostrate bear or mountain lion or sight-ing his rifle, the barrel supported by the stump of his left arm.

The second day at the ranch Ellen took us on the promised hunting trip. She drove me in the buckboard along a pair of wheel tracks that wound for miles through the cedars and then out to a lonely expanse of plain. Willy rode his blue pony, the one they called a grullo. Up near a round treeless mountain, which his mother said was an extinct volcano, she pointed out distant motionless or slowly moving objects which I couldn't make out at first but which gradually took shape for me as small brown living creatures as they moved curiously toward us and then white as they alternately turned and ran.

They still seemed in entire safety from us when Ellen suddenly stopped the horse, passed the lines to me, drew a rifle from beneath the seat, stood up in the buckboard, and fired. The lunge of the horse threw her back into the seat, but not too quickly to keep me from seeing one of the inquisitive brown-and-white wraiths drop to the range while the others fled. When we reached it, I found a beautiful small deerlike creature lying on the grass with blood running from its mouth and from a well-directed hole in its graceful head.

It seemed incredible to me that destruction had

occurred so accurately and at such a great distance.
I had always wanted a rifle of my own to knock over
prairie dogs rearing by their sandy burrows, and I
didn't understand at first why Ellen's splendid
shooting should bother me. Turning, I saw Willy a
few yards away sitting motionless on his pony staring at the dead antelope.

Still in the saddle, he held his mother's unquiet
horse while she had me help her lift the game to the
back of the buckboard, where the bleeding head
was left hanging over the edge. Then we drove back
to the ranch house. It was very strange. Our hunting had been successful. This was exactly what we
wanted, what we had come out to the ranch for, and
yet some inexplicable shadow for me had fallen over
the sunlit plain.

WE STAYED at the ranch for nearly two weeks, school or no school, and if it was a bit long for me, it was short for Willy and his mother. Just how the news that Ellen was home traveled over the wide uninhabited region, I don't know, but the Piños came visiting from Embudo Canyon and the Xavier Oteros from what they called the Red Lake region. Tom Dold and Doc Gammel journeyed out from town for both weekends along with Cousin Albert, and evenings were lively with late dinners, wine, and cards, the days with horses, hunting, and game.

I was glad to get away, especially from the game dinners and the dead antelope and deer hanging in a row in the cold dry air out of reach of the dogs and sun. Town had become somehow peaceful and civilized in my mind, and when we drove back through Ojo Canyon to the East Mesa I felt escape from something, I didn't know quite what. Even the air seemed free again, and it gave me a wonderful feeling to see Moro lying far below us, hardly distinguishable at this distance except for the wisp of black smoke hanging above it from the invisible railroad.

Town seemed even better as we drove into Audiencia Street and the plaza. Then we came to the white house on La Placita and saw workmen laying brick between the two houses.

"What in the world are they doing?" Ellen asked Chepa and Epifania, who rushed out when they saw us.

They seemed agitated and confused.

"It is to be a wall, señora," Chepa said.

"What in heaven for?"

"Señora! Doña Ana and Felicitas daren't come over any more! Not even Suplicante! They must stay over there and we must stay over here. As long as we live."

"It is to be a high wall, señora," Epifania said.

"Seven feet up and from street to alley, Suplicante told us."

Ellen did not ask who had ordered this. We all knew. She said nothing for the moment, but as we went into the house I caught a glimpse of her face, and her cheeks and eyes were frightening.

"I didn't tell you," Cousin Albert said when he came home from the courthouse, "because I didn't want to spoil your holiday. It would have upset you more than it's worth. It may turn out to be not too bad. Snell is having his revenge now. He's working off his temper. In fact, it might turn out to be a good thing."

I often thought later on how tragically wrong he was. Perhaps he knew it even then. He may have been trying to put the best possible face on a blight that would be evident to everyone in Moro and for miles around. Certainly I was only a boy and saw it. Could it be that nothing dared be said outright about Ellen at the trial; that it was not the Western code to accuse a lady so darkly? But now, without breaking the code, without saying a word, Beasley was giving notice that he didn't feel her a fit associate for his wife and children, who were her own sister, niece, and nephew.

What Ellen thought I do not know. More than once while the men were at work on the wall, and

especially when her brother-in-law came out to
look it over, I saw her eyes like agates and that familiar, hard, curiously smaller look on her face like
a tightly nailed but attractive box.

It was gone and in its place a kind of gay des-
peration when friends called.

"Do you know you take your life in your hands
to come? We're in quarantine and under siege, you
know," she'd greet guests in the playful way they
all knew so well. Her dinners were too late in the
evening for Willy and me. We ate our supper much
earlier, but in our room we could hear her poke fun
at her brother-in-law and his wall.

"It's a pity you can't see it by daylight. You
know how Snell is. He won't hire Anglo bricklayers.
They cost too much. No, he hires Abundio Sais and
his brother, Ascensión, who never laid anything but
dobes. Now, we all know that dobes take no mortar,
so Abundio forgets the mortar for one brick and
Ascensión forgets the mortar for another, and the
next round Abundio has to put on abundio mortar
and Ascensión has to give his brick more ascension,
and that's the way it goes, more abundio and ascension, till the wall looks like the stripes of a zebra."

After the laughter, her voice came again, mockingly.

"But Albert's going to talk to Snell. Perhaps

he'll graciously let us cover up our side with adobe.
Then it will be easier to abide it."

Of course, we knew that she would never have
Cousin Albert ask Snell and that, no matter what
was done to the wall, never could she abide it. Most
every evening since we came back she either had
guests at the house or was a guest in some other.
But days were a trial to her. Many an afternoon
we came home from school and found Critter hitched
up in front of the house, with Ellen at the door,
hatted and coated to take us for a ride.

Once the buggy wheels rolled clear of town, you
could feel her other self return, her old self, the one
I liked best. We drove all the roads and lanes
through the irrigated small ranches along the river,
and the more populated roads through the native
villages of Yrisarri and Gutierreztown. But mostly
Ellen took the wheel tracks that crossed and criss-
crossed, wheeled and looped, on the mesa. There
were two mesas, one across the river, another across
the railroad. Here the range rolled and dipped and
curled and was cut by all sorts of dry watercourses
so that the trails skirted the edge of deep draws, and
where you could look across wide cañadas.

It wasn't only to get away from town that she
went, I think, but to be driving Critter. There was
a certain relationship between Ellen and her horse

that only those who ride or drive horses can understand today. It may be that he was a link to her
dead father, as Dr. Gammel once claimed, but the
brute was close to her in his own right, much closer
than I, for example, a silent companion on the
empty desolate spaces, one who never failed her, and
much stronger than any of us so that when he
obeyed and did her will, she drew from his strength
as well as from her own.

But at dusk when we got back to the house, the
wall was always there, not an idle rumor that could
be lived down and forgotten, rather a monument
pointing as long as it stood. Words you could reply
to and criminal charges could be refuted in court,
but how would you answer or disprove an evil brick
wall? Every day when town and ranch folk went by,
there it was to see and remember, reviving the dark
whispers.

I think it was when she couldn't stand the wall
any more that she would drive to the ranch, and
that was why during the holidays we went to Rancho
Antiguo. But she always gave other reasons for
going.

"Wouldn't you like a white Christmas?" she
asked as we walked home from midnight Mass. "The
only snow this year is up in La Sierra. How would
you like to run up and see the Pereas?"

She made it sound so easy, as if it were only an hour's drive, but I knew the Greenhorns, which she called La Sierra, were forty miles away and the ranch of the Pereas must be farther. The morning we left, Moro was still in shadow but far to the north the sun was already red on the snowy summits. Critter kept up his incredible trot all the way except now and then on the grades when he slipped back into a running walk.

"He's resting when he does that," Willy informed me. "It's the Indian shuffle."

I had never seen anyone received as Ellen was at Rancho Antiguo, like someone of royal family. I suspected the Pereas seldom saw visitors up here near the Colorado border, but next day guests came from Trinidad and they treated her the same. The men surrounded her, drawing out her talk and laughter. The women did the unheard-of Spanish act of listening, and children watched her in a kind of wondering worship.

Long after Willy and I went to bed in a huge room with others younger than we were, we could hear her laugh next door in the old sala, a particular kind of laugh I seldom hear today except among women and girls of Spanish blood or among those who learned it from them, a series of quick, tiny, almost incoherent explosions, tumbling out all at once like mixed-up notes of music, without rhyme or reason, very virgencita, contagious, and delightful to hear.

But if Ellen was looked up to at the Pereas', Critter was not. The Perea family was noted for raising white sheep and black horses. Any colt of another color was promptly sold, and they had no use for Critter's oscuro shade. "It's the color of the dirt," they said. Also, their horses were their chattels, not their friends. They reined them high and trained them to walk and prance in style. Critter's lounging ways, the low posture of his head, and his indifference to showing spirit to order invited their contempt.

Moreover, Critter declined to graze away with the other horses, but hung around close to the ranch house, cropping what grass he could find. He seemed concerned about us in this strange place. The first time Willy went to the excusado, or water closet, the grand like of which there was nothing outside at the Johnson y Campo ranch, he did not come out for a long time. Critter kept grazing closer. Finally he ambled up, pushed the door open with his nose, stuck his head in, and looked around. It was, Ellen said afterward, as if he wanted to see what this place was and what Willy was doing in it. This excited the Pereas' huge amusement and their remarks nettled Ellen.

"Why are you such a baby?" she scolded Critter. "You won't stay with the other horses. You have to hang around me like a spoiled child around its mother."

Whether he understood her, I have no notion. He looked back at her calmly, then went on grazing, but Ellen was plainly impatient with him. So he couldn't follow us when we went to the mountains, she had him put in a corral. We saw him looking after us as we drove away to scenery more beautiful than I knew existed. The crowning point of the trip was a grassy trail through a high valley called Canyon de Espíritu Santo, or Holy Ghost Canyon, where the blue firs and red-boled pines drooped with moss and a crystal cold river rushed down from a snowy peak at the head of the canyon.

We came back elated from our trip, but the first thing we heard as we neared the ranch was Critter whinnying at us from where he stood with his head over the corral fence.

Early next morning I felt a hand shake me under the heavy blankets spun from native fleeces. It was Ellen saying that we must go. Sleepily Willy begged to stay another day.

"No, it's impossible," his mother said. "We could be snowed in for weeks up here."

When we sat up we saw through the dim window what looked like fine bits of gray wool slowly falling to the ground as I had often seen them shaken to the floor of the hide building at the commission house. The ground already lay covered, and when we left we could see our tracks deep in the white road. We could also see the Pereas standing on the portal waving after us, while far above and behind them on the mountainsides gusts of white swirled over the firs and pines.

We ourselves didn't feel the force of the wind till we left the shelter of the mountains. Coming to the mouth of the canyon, we could see in front of us the white particles driven almost horizontally from the northwest. Critter saw them, too. His ears pricked, and when the wind reached him, tossing his mane, he answered with doubled speed.

Willy laughed. "He doesn't like it, Mama."

"I hope it stings him," his mother said. "He's been a very temperamental boy."

At first it was pleasant enough racing through the snow, but after an hour or two it had grown much colder and the snow was thicker and finer, a solid white curtain closing us in. The rolling foot-hills that had been so pleasant when we came through them a few days before were blotted out and the road with them.

"How do we know where we are?" Willy wondered.

I guessed that Ellen knew no more than we did, but she answered at once. "San Antonio knows."

"He might have forgotten us here in the Arriba country," Willy pointed out.

"No," she promised confidently, "I told Father Goshard I'd get a new robe for San Antonio, the best China silk and a gold hem. If we get lost up here in the snow, San Antonio knows he'd never get it."

I gazed at Ellen curiously. Sometimes when the Spanish came out in her, she surprised me.

The cold by now was intense. We huddled under what blankets we had, the rubber shield of the buggy buttoned up tight from dash to top with the reins passing through a slit. The isinglass peekholes were almost constantly blinded with snow except when a jolt from the wheels or our hands would clear them. But when we looked out, all we could see was the brown furry shape of Critter, a tiny moving island in the midst of a white wilderness with neither sky above nor solid ground beneath.

Only once did I see anything besides Critter and his frozen breath. That was when we passed close to a landmark strange to me, a lone butte like a giant idol with a tree growing out of its head. I could remember passing no such object on the way up. For a moment the butte stood there revealed, then fresh waves of white blotted it out. But it couldn't blot out a terrible conviction from my mind. For the last hours Ellen had made no attempt to guide Critter, letting him choose his own way in the barren waste. Now I knew that he must be lost. More than once his trot dragged to a walk and we could feel the snow pushing against the buggy box. Sometimes he frightened us by stopping altogether. Peering out, we watched him rub one side of his head, then the other against the ends of the shafts. Ellen said she thought he was rubbing the icicles from his eyes, a remark which sobered me. After this he went on, but sooner or later, I felt, the snow must stop him and bury us in its depths.

The day dragged, growing no lighter. It seemed a week since we had left the Pereas and even since we ate the lunch they had packed for us. Suddenly Ellen startled us by her cry. Looking out of the peephole, I saw what appeared to be a wide gray streak in the snow. It ran at right angles to our course and disappeared into the blizzard.

"You wonderful thing!" she screamed. I thought at first she called to this mysterious outline on the white earth. Then I realized it had been to Critter. "It's the Baca road!" she told us. "He never took the road to town. He's brought us down behind the Prietas straight for the ranch."

As if recognition of the familiar landmark raised his spirits also, the brown furry shape, almost black now with sweat, stepped up his pace. Down here there seemed to be less snow. We learned afterward that it had started to fall much later at the ranch. We reached places where the wind had left our trail almost bare, and here Critter let himself go. He had been dragging a heavy buggy with three people through snow and often drifts for hours. By all accounts he should have been worn out, brought to one of those violent trembling spells that in a Western horse mean exhaustion and death. But now his legs fairly flew. The stable and alfalfa ahead seemed to tap new energies in his being. I had never seen a horse lay himself so close to the ground, as if to spare every inch of up-and-down motion.

There was great excitement at the ranch when we arrived. They hadn't known we had ever left town. Mama Grande, aroused by the commotion, called demandingly from the portal that we come in at once. But Ellen refused to go until she saw Critter cared for. He steamed in the frosty air like a railroad engine on a zero morning. When I climbed

stiffly to the ground I saw that not a hair on his
body but was laid, curled, twisted with sweat and
wind.

Fidel came running to take over the unhitching
and lead him to his stall. The hay that we thought
he had run for lay plentiful in his manger, but now
that he had reached it, there was no effort to touch
it. He stood with hoofs somewhat far apart, head
down, his ice-and-snow-rimmed eyes paying attention to none of us, as if what he wanted most in the
world was just to stand there and never move. This
was how he stayed while Fidel and Teofilo rubbed
him down.

All this time Mama Grande, bundled up in a great
woolen rebozo, stood in the entry chattering angrily,
bombarding Ellen with questions, calling God's
wrath down on the Pereas for letting us go, while
swarthy faces nodded intently behind her. Once
Fidel spoke in support of her. His strong brown
weathered face was grave.

"Dios was with you, Doña Ellen," he said. "The
snow drifts worse on the Moro road. Deep as a
house sometimes. Had Critter gone that way, never
maybe would you have got through."

It was late in the evening when he brought word
to the house.

"It is well now. Critter has started to eat."

vi

THE BLIZZARD did something to Ellen. I never knew
exactly what. Perhaps it was Critter that did it.
Perhaps it had been the close call of death, not so
much on her as on Willy. As she drove us back to
town I felt her definitely changed from the person
who had driven us to Rancho Antiguo. At home,
confronted by the wall, I was aware of bitter
emotions working in her again, but once inside of
the house she seemed to master and hide them. In the
days that followed I noticed that she avoided the

wall, staying in parts of the house where it couldn't be seen, sewing with her own fingers the promised robe for San Antonio and taking it to church several times to measure and fit.

The second week she called Willy.

"I want you to go over to your Tía Ana for me. Say I hope they can come to dinner Saturday evening. It will be just family, theirs and ours. Of course, I expect Uncle Snell and Felicitas. Say I hope Felicitas can stay up for the evening."

I could feel Willy's slow surprise.

"Do you think they'll come?"

"Well, we know they've come before. After all, Ana is my sister and Felicitas your blood cousin. We love them and I'm sure they love us."

Willy stared at his mother. This was a new Ellen, one I had never seen before, and evidently Willy hadn't either.

"But do you think he'll let her?"

"He should—if we think of him with charity and kindness. Charity and kindness can do wonders, Father Goshard says, even to Snell Beasley. You and Jud must treat him with love, Willy, when you see him."

"How do you mean?" Willy looked dismayed.

"Talk and act toward him like nothing had happened, as if he never sent his herd up Ojo Canyon.

If we treat him with love, then perhaps everything will be all right."

Once we were outside, Willy made a face to me, a face of wonder and things unspoken as only those of Latin blood can. Reluctantly he took his way toward the forbidden wall and then behind it, keeping me close beside him. I could see that he was uneasy. When Felicitas sprang out at us in the patio, he fairly jumped.

"Willy Sessions! You better get out of here!" she threatened.

Willy seemed relieved if anything by the encounter.

"I don't need to get out," he stammered. "Mama says we love you and you love us and everything is going to be all right."

The girl stared at him. She moved up and planted herself directly in front of him.

"What did you say, Willy?"

"Felicitas!" Willy implored her. "Do me the favor. Go and tell your mother for Mama. Tell her that we love you and you love us and she wants you over for dinner Saturday night. Uncle Snell, too."

"You better go, Willy Sessions, before Papa comes home and hears you."

"Felicitas!" Willy begged. "Do me the favor. Just tell your mama for Mama. Tell her—"

Felicitas put her fingers over her ears.

"I don't hear you," she chanted. "I don't hear you. I didn't hear a word you said."

Willy looked at me. His face was haggard. He considered his aunt's brick house like a prisoner the gibbet.

"Come along in, Jud!" he begged. "Whatever you do, stand by me. Don't run off."

I could see that he was afraid. Slowly he pushed open the side door and went in with me close behind. There looking at us, as frightened as we, stood his aunt. I think she had been watching from the window.

"Tía Ana!" Willy cried, grateful to see her, and stammered out his mother's invitation.

He spoke incoherently. I could hardly understand him, but she must have, for she startled us by bursting into tears. She hugged him and cried over him, then pushed him aside and looked quickly out of the window.

"Now you better go, Willy. Tell your mother a thousand thanks. Tell her I have a day to think about. I'm afraid that we can't come next Saturday. Maybe not the next either. But one of these Saturdays God will smile and it will be all right. Then we will come and I will let her know."

When Cousin Albert came home, Ellen told him.

Cousin Albert nodded. I noticed that he looked at her gravely, as if this was a strange Ellen, she who used to make light and poke fun at such things. But if he had judicial reservations, he kept them to himself. After all, she was the child of several races, with long lines of conflicting ancestors rising in her from the past for a moment or two before falling back into the rich and ancient blood stream. To me, an Anglo boy from Missouri without a drop of the blood of the conquerors or of the English gentry in his veins, Ellen seemed still more of that mysterious creature, a lady, with all the contradictions and complexities of her sex.

What puzzled and almost awed me was the stretch of peace and content in the house that followed Ellen's offer of love. Even the icy heart of winter seemed mellowed by some unknown beneficent influence. I had never seen a gentler January in Moro, with temperate days and a great balminess to the air. The snowfall of some weeks ago had long since melted. The moisture had soaked into the ground, where next spring, everyone agreed, it would produce abundant grass on the range. Despite frost at night, both banks were fringed all winter with green along the river, and the laguna in the Big Bosque had the placidity of September. I could sit there on an old cottonwood log of a late January or

early February day and, warmed by the sun, imagine it almost summer with the tule growing lux-
uriantly around it, with redwing blackbirds riding
the bent cattails and some rare waterfowl swimming
from the depths of the green reeds.

But the Beasleys never sent word about the dinner. Ellen kept Saturday evenings open for them,
and when they did not come Willy and I would stay
up to eat with her. Cousin Albert was at court in
San Ysidro County. On this certain Saturday night,
I remember, we were to have sopapillas for dessert,
a sweet hollow puff fried like a doughnut, of which
I was very fond. I never got enough of them. We
were still at the mutton when we became aware of
excitement in the kitchen. I had heard Ellen warn
Epifania several times against loud kitchen talk
while we were at the dinner table. Now her cheeks
flushed slightly as it kept up, but she said nothing.
Then the kitchen door opened and Teofilo from
the ranch burst into the dining-room.

"Dios nos ayuda, patrona!" he groaned. "God
help us, mistress!" and fell down on his knees by
the side of Ellen's chair.

I had never seen anything like this, a grown man
such as Teofilo acting like a grief-stricken child to
a mother younger than he. But it was apparent
from Ellen's and Willy's faces, as well as from those

of Epifania and Chepa looking in from the kitchen door, that all was perfectly regular.

"What is it, Teo?" Ellen asked. "Is it Doña Sofía!"

"No, gracias á Dios."

"Is it Don Carlos?"

He ducked his head lower as if a sensitive spot had been touched.

"He is the one, patrona."

"Is he living?"

"Thanks to God, when I left. But the holes in him are deep and he lost much blood."

"Blood!" Something hard and ugly had come into Ellen's voice. We all felt it, including Teofilo. Before saying more, he got to his feet as if what he was about to tell would be blasphemy from his knees.

Once on his feet, the story came out swiftly and with such passionate hissing of sibilants and rolling of r's that it was difficult for me to follow. But I understood enough—how Charley had started that afternoon for town on his regular Saturday-night spree. At the mesa end of the canyon he had met two men on horseback. He didn't know their names but thought he had seen them before and that they hailed from Baca County. They had stopped him and asked if he was Charley Johnson y Campo. Yes, he said, he was. They asked, was he the one who had sworn in court he had shot and killed Frank Jeffcoat. Yes, Charley said, he guessed he had. Then they pulled their revolvers and fired on him and galloped off. Charley himself told all this an hour later to the sheepherder who discovered him and who had run to the ranch with the news. When Fidel and others got there, they found their patrón still in the buggy. Except for jumping a few feet to one side, his well-trained horse hadn't moved.

When I looked at Ellen, the new gentleness of the last weeks had wholly vanished. Her blue eyes were almost black.

"Run for Dr. Gammel. Send him to the ranch. Tell him to hurry."

"The doctor is already gone, patrona," Teofilo said. "I stopped at his house first. Doña Sofía said that is the way I must do it."

"Then you can help Manuel harness Critter. I will drive out myself as soon as I change my clothes."

Before she could get away, Fidel arrived from the ranch with another smoking horse and the word that Charley was dead. He had met the doctor on the mesa and told him, but the good señor doctor said he was the coroner and had to go anyhow. Besides, Doña Sofía would probably need him. But he was relieved he would not have to push his horse now. He would stay at the ranch till tomorrow.

Epifania and Chepa acted like stricken nuns, and Manuel was a subdued mountain of flesh. Even Fidel, one of the most competent and self-reliant Mexicans I ever knew, was much affected. But if Ellen mourned, it was in secret. Her cool English blood seemed to disengage itself from the warm Spanish blood and take charge. She dispatched Manuel for Amado Martínez. The door to the second parlor was shut while she talked to the sheriff. All I heard was his promise to send a telegram to Cousin Albert when he left.

Ellen drove Willy and me to the ranch. Once we had left town, she seemed more Spanish than English. The cry of grief with which she and Mama Grande greeted each other sounded almost foreign to me, as did the velorio del defunto a night or two later in the big house, with the natives coming in and sitting on benches around the white walls, the songs of death and sorrow, murder and revenge, and the supper served with the inevitable café and vino. All the time the corpse lay in a coffin of pine boards made by the ranch carpenter and covered with black cloth, his blond hair and English features looking out of place here amid the foreign talk and songs and dark faces.

Willy was my whispering informant, telling me
who everyone was. The singer was called the rezador,
paid to sing and paid to stop. The glum-looking
man on the end of his bench was Noé Vigil, whose
jokes and pranks were told all over the sheep range.
The woman by the coffin was old Josefina, so ancient that she addressed Willy's grandmother as
niña, "child." The one next to her they called the
Chicken Woman because she had come to work at
the ranch house with a chicken under her arm, saying it had laid her an egg when she had nothing to
eat and she wouldn't stay if the chicken couldn't.
Mama Grande had had the chicken secretly done
away with, for how could she keep a chicken in the
house?—and the woman had searched for it all day
and then cried all night.

Services for Uncle Charley were held in the ranch
chapel, with Father Goshard and priests from Sa-
lado and Tajique in charge. Only the family and important family friends could get into the chapel. It
was a chilly gray day. There was no heat except
from the candles, and it felt cold as a cave, but not
so cold as outside, where more than a hundred Mexicans from the ranch and surrounding region stood
in the bitter wind listening to what sounds of the
Mass came through the open door before the holy

words were caught up and dissipated into the sound-less void.

Services were delayed, waiting for Doña Ana. Not till they had given her up and Father Goshard was at the altar did she come with Beasley. I thought he tried to keep her to the rear, but she slipped up to the front between Ellen and Mama Grande, where she held a hand of each. That was also the way they stood at the grave, while Beasley waited expression-less just behind her. I was next to him and had full opportunity to inspect the man and measure him, to see the dark blood in his temples and the thick immovable way he stood.

It was an unforgettable scene. A desert grave-yard is to me one of the loneliest sights in the world, an expression of man's transience and unimpor-tance on earth, and the Rancho Zelandia cemetery was no exception. The few stone markers had been visibly mended after being twice knocked down by the herd. Wooden crosses, split and broken by hoofs, had been bound by twine. This, with the empty tinsel that Mexicans like to heap on their graves, gave the place a shabby and pitiful air. To me our little group of humans standing there by the open grave looked helpless and insignificant, mere grains of dust against the vast spaces beyond.

How anyone could harbor hate at a time like this, I didn't understand. A short distance from the open grave was the patch of unsanctified desert waste where two or three men slept unblessed and unmarked. Here could be seen the still partially fresh mound of Frank Jeffcoat. His grave and Charley's were not a hundred yards apart. They stood out like unhealed scars from the rest of the landscape, and I wondered how many more lives would be dragged down into the dark and silent earth before it was over.

Willy and I stayed until the last shovelful of dry New Mexican soil was thrown on the coffin. When we turned away, all we could see of Uncle Snell and Aunt Ana was a buggy vanishing up Ojo Canyon.

vii

THERE was difficulty finding the men who had shot and killed Charley. No one had seen two strangers on horseback in the vicinity that day, not even the herder who had first found the wounded man.

But a week later Apolonio Sena, a sheep rancher who had testified for Charley's character at the trial, was shot and killed on his ranch, and this time the men who had done it were recognized and named. They were Grover Reid and Earl Paulson of the Muleshoes in Baca County. Most everyone, I think, felt at once that these were the same men who had done the earlier killing. First there had been two of them, as Charley had said. Then the shooting of Frank Jeffcoat was involved in both cases. Both were outspoken "Jeffcoats," a term we had begun to call cattlemen and their sympathizers. It became a recognized word in Moro and was used in testimony during the trial.

At first most of us were not too excited over the fate of the Apolonio Sena killers. Then we grew aware that there might be more to their trial than we thought. No evidence had turned up to name and try the murderers of Charley, but there was plenty against those of the second victim and if they were the same men in both cases, it didn't matter too much for which crime they were convicted. The important thing was that they be tried and, if guilty, punished. In fact, by the time it came around, the trial of Reid and Paulson became perhaps the most important and significant to take place in the county, not so much for the crime named in the case but because it stood for the more sensational murder never officially mentioned in the trial, that of Charley Johnson y Campo.

The first time I became conscious of possible ugly complications ahead was before the two men had been arrested.

"I hope those two Jeffcoats cleared out for Old Mexico," Tom Dold said to Cousin Albert.

It sounded strange to me from him. I expected Cousin Albert to reply that, no matter who they murdered, the two men should be caught and tried. To my surprise, he turned to Tom with that certain expression on his face which meant, this is in confidence, but you are more right than you know.

"If I wasn't an official sworn to recognize the legal processes," he confided in a low voice, "I'd be tempted to send a friend to suggest that they get out of the country before those processes catch up to them and us all."

Now what made him say that, I wondered, and especially the words "us all"? Whatever his thoughts, I'm sure he said nothing of them to Ellen. She had been hard hit by Charley's murder. She might have made light of Charley in life, become impatient with him as a rancher and been annoyed by his heavy drinking, but his tragedy after his ordeal in court on behalf of her garden, if of nothing more, had affected her harder than I had supposed possible. This was brought home to me when we were back in the house at Moro. Cousin Albert had returned to court in San Ysidro County. That evening Tom Dold, the Kidds, and others were in the sala.

"Well, Paulson and Reid were brought in today," Tom mentioned. "The first thing they wanted was their lawyer."

I saw the quick lift of Ellen's head.

"I should think no decent lawyer in Moro County would be anxious to defend them."

"I'm afraid they hadn't much trouble. They didn't have to go very far."

We all knew whom he meant.

"I'm not surprised," Ellen said bitterly. "I hope you will volunteer your services to help prosecute them."

"My services wouldn't be very welcome, Ellen."

"Well, I shan't rest till both of them are convicted and hung," she answered, and her vehemence surprised me. When I glanced at Willy, his face, usually sallow enough, looked pale.

"The Jeffcoats are saying," Tom went on, "that since Charley was freed by the court, Reid and Paulson should be freed also."

"But Charley didn't go free," Ellen declared swiftly. "He's dead, and that should be the fate of these men, too."

She said it with such passion and devotion to her murdered brother that I felt strong sympathy for her and her cause. Indeed, I thought her admirable as she sat there, faithful, with high principles that

refused to give, and yet very attractive, too. When
the motion was brought by Beasley that Cousin Albert disqualify himself from sitting in the case because of the linking of the two killings in the public
mind, I silently applauded her quiet relentlessness
that, I'm sure, left him no other course than to
insist upon hearing the case himself.

"To abandon the bench in this case would be
deserting your mother," I once heard him tell Willy.
"She'd think it public admission that I thought
these two Jeffcoats had cause to do what they did."

I thought it fine on Ellen's part to bear such an
influence on the court for right and justice. Not till
the Grand Jury had returned an indictment, the
two men had been arraigned, and threatening Jeffcoats from several counties had begun rallying in
their defense did I realize what lay ahead of us—
another ugly and interminable trial, vindictiveness
and more vindictiveness. I saw that the one on whom
the brunt of it would fall was not Ellen so much as
Cousin Albert, who had had little or nothing to do
with it but must stand up for her interest, bringing
in if possible a verdict she would regard as just, and
then endure the storm that must break on him.

That evening I watched him in the wide hall, the
brass reading-lamp pulled down, the Denver paper
in his hands. He looked slight, a small-boned, sen-

sitive-skinned man, and yet there was visible in the
way he sat there, in his slender back and the cut and
projection of his beard, a doughtiness that made
me feel good to have some of the same blood as his
flowing in my veins.

The trial was set for the fall term of court. For
some time I had noticed that Willy was not himself.
In the morning when he first sat up in bed, his face
looked dead white against the heavy black bang that
inevitably came down over his forehead. Ellen had
Dr. Gammel examine him and leave twisted white
papers containing an ugly-tasting powder.

All spring while the peaches and apricots were
in delicate bloom against the raw brown land, when
cottonwoods were budding and the major domo had
his men cleaning out the acequia madre, Willy's
complaint grew no better. The clanking of our wind-
mill in the steady southwest wind seemed to make
him nervous, and when we came upon men standing
or squatting together on the sunny side of buildings
and corral walls, he would give them a wide berth as
if against any mention of the coming trial and
guilts involved. The courthouse he avoided as the
pesthouse. When Cousin Albert was in town and
Ellen sent the boy to his father on an errand, Willy
would ask me to go instead.

"I'll do something for you, Jud," he would say.

There were only two places around Moro that drew him. One was the stable. Here with the strong scent of horses, with Critter's calm presence and the deep sound of his molars grinding hay and corn, Willy would spend hours, talking of horses, sheep, and the ranch, addressing his remarks to Manuel or to me, if I'd listen, getting into the box stall, running his hand over Critter's neck and legs, brushing out his mane and tail. Critter suffered him to do anything, crawl between his legs, lift a foreleg to look at a hoof, or all four legs one after the other, practice leaping up to his bare back, or lead him around the stall by the forelock.

The other place Willy haunted was the Big Bosque. He would bridle Critter. Then he and I would ride him bareback across the river through the unplanted grove of ancient cottonwoods. Here the town disappeared. All we could see were sky and the wide land, the craggy trunks and the rise to the mesa beyond. The grass was already greening up in wet places, and far ahead a violet haze spread over the ground. When you came closer you found it was endless patches of early pink loco in bloom.

Now as I look back I think that Willy felt things ahead that I didn't. He wasn't trying to forget so much as to recapture while there was still time. For this he was given an exceptional summer. Everyone said they had never seen the range greener. When school was finished for another term and we had moved back to the ranch, he cleaved to his saddle like an ax bit to the handle. With Critter and Cousin Albert's buggy team in the stable, there had been no room in town for his pony. Now he made up for it, and I had to ride with him.

There's a blessed amnesia about life in the saddle, especially in the West, that is more like survival in the Elysian Fields than oblivion. Willy had never felt, I think, what I had in the big house in the canyon. To him it was home, the Casa Grande, the house of many rooms. Whenever in the past there had been need of a new room, the Campos had simply laid out more dobe bricks to dry and added the walls they wanted. There were now some twenty-six or -seven rooms, one entering the other or into some small hall, and all built around a central patio shaded by two narrow-leaved mountain cotton-woods. Willy knew every room like the back of his hand. He had been born in one. In the patio he had watched troupes of entertainers and rope dancers from Old Mexico.

But now, I think, sharpened by shock in his own lifetime, Willy had begun to feel the emanation of things long past, dark ancient influences in the house, perhaps shadows cast by the future. We never spoke of them. All I knew was that when we went out of the house, he seemed to feel better, as I did, and that once lifted to our ponies' backs we had freed ourselves for a time from the presence of evil or its power to harm us. Even the patches of cemetery with Frank Jeffcoat's and Charley's graves became at once harmless, something beneath us, to be left far behind. Riding out, we were prisoners suddenly escaped to the unfettered world of land and sky. Before, behind, and beneath us swept the open range, fenceless, seemingly without border or end. This was the older, more joyous world where the Creator and the mark of His hand were still to be seen and felt. We breathed air never before tasted by a human being. We watered our horses in ponds unnamed and unknown except by the tule, wild waterfowl, and the wandering herder. To come on these or on some bright wild garden of range flowers carpeting the ground, blossoms that probably had never before been seen by the human eye and probably would not again, gave us a feeling of the largesse of God and of receiving favors directly from His hand.

Mexican workers, perhaps of necessity, are great ones to rise early. In Old Town I knew them to be up drinking their coffee and getting ready to go about their work when most Anglos were still asleep.

Out on the ranch, lights twinkled in the jacals when all remained dark. With the day coming alive, the natives were ready to live and have a part in it. Willy and I seldom saw the sunrise. Our beds were too snug. The hour we liked best was just before sundown, when the glare of the desert day is gone. Then the soft red sunlight lies on the western slopes of the grassy swells and buttes and the violet light from distant mountains begins to reach out to you and beyond.

Often we loitered in some distant spot so we could ride home through it without talking, just living, our minds closed to civilized things such as courts and houses, open only to the delicious awareness of a more pagan and primitive existence. We watched the evening rite of distant horses, mere specks, grazing peacefully while night came down over them. All the time we were aware of the vistas, the land running on and on. The plains birds, the horned larks and the longspurs, were audible symbols of this endlessness. Almost never could we see them at this hour, only hear their wild plaintive notes that seemed to come out of the air from no apparent direction.

June was the perfect month at our altitude. As the calendar turned to July, the priceless rains

came, especially such rains as used to fall then.
Mornings as a rule were brilliant and clear. Gradually after lunch giant thunderheads would build
up, Himalayan cloud peaks that could be seen for
sixty or eighty miles. Promptly at four o'clock
every day the heavenly irrigation would be turned
on. Mama Grande used to say that you could set
your clock by it. The long mountain thunder rolled
along the Prietas so that for minutes, or so it
seemed, we heard the continuous reverberations of
a single clap. Sometimes it would rain gently all
night. Sometimes it would be over for the day in an
hour or two, in either case leaving a drenched and
fragrant world.

This is the scent more than any other that takes
me back to Willy, the penetrating pungence of wet
cedars. The smell of the sun on dry cedars is something entirely different. Through both wet and
dry cedars Willy and I rode unreckoned miles, the
familiar deep body sounds of our loping horses in
our ears, the moisture from the occasional loud
sneezes pleasantly cooling our faces.

Willy hated, I know, to see the summer days go
by and especially in the cedars. They grew in a
belt two to five miles wide and unnumbered miles
long at the foot of the Prietas, a rolling, sometimes

almost level country of riders' delight. The open range is nearly always the same, the cedar country different, filled with constantly changing scenes. On the open range the rider is conspicuous for miles. In the cedars he is hidden, swallowed up in an endless succession of glades and parks like small clear green lakes of grass where for the distance of a few yards or rods the cedars and pinyons for some unknown reason refuse to grow.

I remember two or three spots Willy showed me that the Mexicans said were evil. They looked to me like any other, patches of grama grass swarming with blue or black seed heads, surrounded by clumps of the dwarf trees.

"Once in the past a very bad thing happened here," Willy told me in a low voice.

"What kind of bad thing?"

"Blood. See, even our ponies know it."

It was true that they didn't like to stop and graze here as they did other places. Willy and I would stay as long as we dared, tasting the sensation of chill. Suddenly, as if some unknown thing was about to burst out of the deformed cedars, we would look at each other, dig our heels into our ponies' sides, and gallop off, heading for the open range where as far as we could see lay the calm peace of the wide spaces.

There was one thing, we were to learn, that we couldn't gallop away from so easily. This was the trial to come, the contest between good and evil, or was it between evil and evil? Anyhow, it lay directly ahead, coming nearer and still nearer each time the sun rose.

◆ *viii* ◆

When we left the ranch in September, the coming trial had already taken over the town. Crossing the mesa, we could see numerous black dots on the public road north of us, indicating an unusual number of rigs and riders converging on Moro. Fall's Wagon Yard near the river looked full, we noticed, as we drove by, and we found the plaza and even some of the narrow streets of Old Town choked with horses and unhitched teams.

It was all the more significant since this was

96

roundup time on the cattle ranches. Of course, some
of the visitors were sheepmen intent on seeing judg-
ment overtake their enemy who had shot down two
of their fellow ranchers in cold blood. But most of
them were cowmen who hated sheep. Their badge
was plain enough to us. The sheepmen might look
wild and rough, but it was more the wild roughness
of an old fleece long worn on the seat of an arm-
chair. I think most of the cowmen knew Judge Session's wife or at least her yellow-top buggy. I noticed that those in the street gazed belligerently at
us as we drove by.

"Pay no attention, muchachos," Ellen said,
"Looks don't kill. We won't perish."

"They carry guns," Willy reminded.

"Yes, you can tell the devil by his hoofs and
horns and the cowman by his spurs and pistols."

Even in the sanctuary of the big white house on
La Placita I could feel the tension in the town. In
this high dry climate of New Mexico, sultriness is
almost unknown. Yet here it was in Moro, an op-
pression that did not pass like a storm in a matter
of hours but hung black over the mesa for days,
gathering force and fervor until it should finally
break and discharge its burden on those beneath.

Ellen must have felt it as I did, but reveled in it.
This was the Spanish in her, responding to crowds,

emotion, and suspense. Anyone could see now that
the trial concerned more than justice to Apolonio
Sena. The house had never been so filled since I
knew it. First Mama Grande came in for the dura-
tion. Then ranching friends of the family visited
while attending the trial, the Pereas from La Sierra,
and others I had never seen before. The front part
of the house buzzed and bombilated with them, and
a constant hum came from the rear. Fidel had
brought Piedad, a maid, along with Mama Grande,
and Teofilo had driven a ranch wagon to town with
Mama Grande's tremendous leather brassbound
trunk and the carcasses of several sheep for the
table.

This time Willy and I were not required to go to
the trial, but hardly a detail was spared our young
ears. News from the courtroom reached our kitchen
and stable as quickly and sometimes quicker than
it did the two parlors. At dinner and supper the
long cloth-covered plank table in the dining-room
supported a lively discussion of the trial in general and the last session in detail and particular. At
the head of the table, on her rawhide-seated chair
overlaid with a scarlet cushion to raise her a little,
Ellen reigned over her court, never letting it get out
of hand, injecting lightness and wit when it became
too serious, bringing it back to proper decorum

when it grew too lively, delivering the crowning comment on the person or thing under discussion.

"There are two places," she would say, "where, no matter how dull, we must listen and never interrupt or ask questions or argue. One is in church." Everyone would laugh at Father Goshard if he was there. "The other is in court," and then the laughter would be at Cousin Albert.

"I am old, yes," she would sometimes sigh. She looked to be in her twenties at such a time and yet I knew she must be ten years older to have had Willy. "But, praise to God, Señora Vargas" (naming an aged crone) "is older than I."

Not all of her comments were light.

"That child of double adultery," I heard her say once, a phrase which made my hair stand on end.

To my surprise, the name of the lawyer who defended the murderers was never mentioned. But a great deal was said about el culebrón, "the large snake," and it took me some time to realize that this was their name for Snell Beasley, and then I understood the scorn, contempt, and sometimes hissing with which the word was spoken.

Cousin Albert would say little or nothing about the case. At times he inserted a few calming sentences, often in English, which in itself had the effect of dignity and restraint.

"Ask me a month from now," he'd say when appealed to for some opinion bearing on the trial. "Today I'm just a piece of furniture pulled up to Ellen's table. I don't hear and I don't speak."

He spoke Spanish well enough but with a Missouri accent like mine. Neither of us could ever hope to equal Willy, who, raised in the language, had only to let the Spanish flow out of him like his breath, belying his three-quarters Anglo blood. His pronunciation of words like "guarniciones," almost like a guttural clearing of the throat, ever excited my admiration.

The only time Willy and I had to attend the trial was when Cousin Albert sentenced the killers. A verdict of first-degree murder had been brought in by the sheepman jury, a great victory for the prosecution. Only Willy and his father didn't seem to share in the triumph, not even when the verdict was upheld and appeal for a new trial denied. As far as Cousin Albert was concerned, it seemed unfortunate because, of all the participants, he had had the hardest time, hearing the endless testimony and arguments, ruling on allegations, statements, and motions for dismissal, silencing the angry demonstration of the Jeffcoats from time to time, and keeping the case generally in hand. Now at the sentencing he looked very formidable, his black

beard and stern eyes frightening me a little from
the bench as he gazed at the two prisoners standing
in the box.

"Grover Reid and Earl Paulson, like other citizens of this territory you enjoyed the privileges of
life, liberty, and the pursuit of happiness. You
watched the grass green in the spring and the young
calves leap. But you were unsatisfied, and cruelly
and forever deprived a fellow citizen of the said
life and pursuit of happiness, one Apolonio Diego
Luis Felipe Sena. You are now remanded to the cus-
tody of Sheriff Martínez to be returned to your
cells, and on Friday, February twentieth, you will
be taken to the jail yard and duly hanged by the
neck until dead."

The words and the way he spoke them sent a chill
along my spine. He turned and glanced down into
the packed court. I fancied he was looking at me,
but immediately knew his eyes were on Ellen near
by. For a moment something passed between them.
His look seemed to say he had vindicated her trust
in him and delivered the murderers not only of
Apolonio Sena but also probably of her brother to
their proper end. Then I thought he looked suddenly tired as he turned away.

"Well, thank the Lord they'll get theirs," I said
to Willy in Spanish as we went out.

He didn't answer, and when we reached the bright New Mexican winter sunlight I saw that he kept his face away.

Ellen had wanted to give a supper party that evening in celebration, but Cousin Albert over-ruled it. He said it would look unseemly and if she held it he wouldn't attend. It was the first time I heard him take such a firm stand in opposition to her and I thought the ordeal of the trial had steeled him. To my surprise, she did not mock or disregard him.

"Whatever you think, Albert," she said.

From this time on I thought I detected a change in their relationship. Up to now Cousin Albert had been the one to come to her.

"Are you all right?" his solicitude had seemed to say. "Can I do anything for you?"

He used to stand waiting a long time just to see her come out of her room or into the sala. Now it was she who came to him. Was he all right? Could she or Epifania do anything for him? And when there was nothing else, she would set herself to entertain and amuse him, to put him in a happier mood. Usually she would act out her story, talk like some person we all knew, intersperse her chatter with amusing exclamations like "Caram-bambamba!" which was a burlesquing of "caramba"

and much like saying "phooey" or "fiddle-faddle."
She had such charm with it, Latin ways of play-
fully crinkling her young face that no one could resist and Cousin Albert didn't try. He would sit in
his chair watching her, listening to her mocking
voice, his face faintly warmed by the picture he
saw and the contradictions and laughter he heard.
But when he left or she turned away, I noticed that
the grave melancholy returned.

I thought at first that her increased affection for
him was gratitude, payment in her kind for his
justice in avenging Charley, but later I was not
so sure. I knew that some cattlemen were still in
the town and heard that they had made threats
against us.

"You can't stop the bull from bellowing," Ellen
said.

But one night after the sentence, men on horseback came riding up La Placita in the early hours
of the morning, shot out the plate-glass windows of
both front parlors, and rode out again, yelling and
shooting into the air. It took several days to get
fresh glass shipped by train from Pueblo, and this
time Ellen did not say "Carambambamba!" She
gave Willy and me strict orders to stay off the street
except on our way to and from school. Mama
Grande grew alarmed and would let Ellen go no-

where on foot. Only Cousin Albert went his usual way, marching his doughty figure twice daily to his court chambers.

All the time the hanging grew closer. Since early fall Willy had had a cold. Romadizo, or hay fever, some would call it today, but you didn't get hay fever in the middle of winter, not until late February or early March when the foothill sabinos sent their powdery pollen on the breeze. Soon Willy grew untalkative even to me. At night he sweated like a colt that had eaten loco weed, and I helped him change to a dry sleeping-garment the night after Manuel told us that the two godless savages had been finally hung, after refusing to kneel with the executioner and preacher when the latter prayed for them.

Now I expected the full fury of the cattlemen to be directed against us. For several nights Willy and I lay listening for the quiet of our Old Town street to be broken. Nothing happened. The hangman's victims were duly buried in the Protestant cemetery. The last cattlemen who had stayed for the execution, we were told, drifted back to their ranches in Baca and San Ysidro counties.

"It's all over now, gracias á Dios," Mama Grande said and went home to the ranch.

But I wasn't so sure. Once Tom Dold came to see

Ellen when Cousin Albert wasn't at home. I noticed they were closeted behind closed doors. What they talked about I didn't know. Twice a day she seemed to grow restless until Cousin Albert would return from the courthouse. Long before his usual hour she began looking for him, extraordinary in someone so self-contained and active as she.

"Did you see my sewing?" she would ask if caught in the act, or else her prayerbook, which surprised me, for only on occasion I saw her sew and almost never found her with her prayerbook.

Term of court at Moro was over now. Next on the calendar was the spring term in Baca County. No railroad had then reached Porvenir, and to get there from Moro meant a three days' journey by buggy. Some earlier judges in the territory had ridden the circuit horseback and many stories were told about them. But more roads, such as they were, had come into use today and Cousin Albert made his rounds with Dan and Choppo in his black pole buggy.

"Will you do me a favor, Albert?" Ellen asked him at the dining-table one day.

"Gladly, if I can," he told her.

"Ask Judge Otero to take over Baca this spring." He looked startled.

"Judge Otero? But how could I do that?"

"You could say you were indisposed." And when

he looked pained, "You must be very tired. You've had a long and difficult ordeal."

"I am a little tired, yes," he admitted, "but not indisposed."

"It's the same thing. Wouldn't you do it for me?" she begged. Her face and eyes were so soft and helpless upon him I didn't see how he could resist.

Cousin Albert looked profoundly disturbed.

"I would do anything for you, Ellen, anything within reason. This, I'm afraid, is impossible. Judge Otero and many others would think me afraid."

It was the word "afraid" that suddenly betrayed to me what she was driving at, revealed as by a blinding light the specter that haunted the back of Ellen's mind. For a moment I could see the wild uninhabited region he must traverse on his way to Baca County, the lonely canyons he must pass through, the remote mesas to be crossed and dry stream beds to be threaded, where the sudden sound of thunder echoing among the barren cliffs and hills might not be heard by another human ear and where a trail might lie for days abandoned except to wild things and stray cattle.

For about a week I didn't hear Ellen bring up the matter again.

"Will you take Willy with you, Albert?" she suddenly begged him the day before he left.

"Willy?" He drew back. "Ellen, you ask the most impractical things."

"Why is it impractical? A change often helps a cold. You know how miserable he's been." She saw him hesitate and pushed her advantage. A very torrent of Spanish words and a woman's reasoning ensued. Now when I glance back I think I can read her thought, her realization that it was she who had got him into the position from which there was no retreat, and this was her last resort to protect him. Her intuition told her that not even the most hardened of men would fire on a buggy if it contained a young boy. Her religious faith was small and her theology smaller, but it may be she believed that if like Abraham she would offer her son as a sacrifice, Dios would not take the life of one so innocent and unsinful.

"I cannot do it, Ellen," Cousin Albert declared. "If I did—"

"This time I will not let you go," Ellen interrupted. "If you won't take him, you must take me!"

I knew then, by her emotion, and Cousin Albert knew too, that she meant it. I knew also that if there was one thing a man hated, it was to hide behind a woman's petticoats. He considered a long time and his face was pale, but in the end he agreed reluctantly to her demand.

Willy's eyes lighted when his mother told him, and the first color in some weeks came to his face. He looked half cured already and pleaded that I be permitted to go along. No, that would put too big a burden on his father, Ellen told him, and, besides, surely he wanted me to stay and look after her? He did not protest too much then. You could see he was wild with excitement over the chance to be with his father, to be free from school and out in the range country he loved. There would be mountains and canyons he had never laid eyes on. But, most of all, he would be away from Moro, would leave the hanging and the two fresh graves behind him.

Court in Baca County was to open Monday morning. Willy and his father left the previous Wednesday in the black buggy. Manuel brought it around in front of the house in the morning. A scattering of local people came to wish the judge well and see him off. Among them was George Atkins, the druggist, with his camera and tripod.

I have an enlarged print of the scene he snapped on the plate that day. It hangs framed and faded on my wall. Beyond the buggy and horses you can see some of the curious witnesses and anxious well-wishers. A few Mexican women have black rebozos over their heads, and some of the men wear boots over their trousers, not the fancy short dress boots worn today but the long, rough, genuine Western boot that reached to the knee.

Of course, the center of attraction in the photograph is Dan and Choppo, the blood bays, a matched pair except for Choppo's white nose. Both horses' heads are high. The blinders flap wide of their eyes. Their harness looks heavy and coarse compared to the tan harness that Ellen used on Critter. In the picture Dan has one front foot raised, pawing to go. In the buggy holding the reins sits Cousin Albert, his back slender and straight, his black beard covering the black strings of the tie he generally wore, his hat not the ten-gallon one of today but the Western hat worn then with a narrow brim and a high crown. Beside him sits Willy looking happier than any photographer before had been able to snap him.

I am not on the picture, having stood behind George Atkins to watch him pop in and out of the black cloth, and there is only a trace of Ellen's skirt on the photograph. But I have a vivid memory of her standing just inside the gate, her face colorless, her white fingers fluttering, her eyes straining after the buggy until it turned and vanished into the plaza.

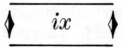

ix

THERE are a few small things we know now about
Cousin Albert's and Willy's journey on the circuit.
It is one of the most famous cases in New Mexican
personal history. People still talk about it. But we
knew almost nothing then.

With the others gone, Ellen left for the ranch in
the morning. She did not ask me along. Of course,
I had my school, but she seemed to have forgotten
me. The day before, she had been restless, almost
feverish. This morning she was calmer. Her travelers had been on their way a full day now. She had

done what she could to prevent Cousin Albert from going. Failing in that, she had sent Willy to insure his safety on the way.

A week later when she came back from the ranch, she seemed like her old self. The period of suspense was over. Cousin Albert's trip to Baca County took only three days at most. He must have arrived long since and everything was all right.

I suppose I looked a little forlorn.

"Pobrecito!" she said. "I shouldn't have left you alone in the house. You suffer like me with Willy away."

That evening at dinner she tried to make up for her neglect.

"You missed the trip with Willy. Now I must tell you some things you missed. The country is nothing much. But the people make up for it. The first night you would have stayed with the Romeros. There is Cosme. He doesn't count. The all-important are his four sisters. They are the priceless ones. What one says, the others must say, too. Everything is said four times. It is like an echo. It runs all around the room. Oye, oye, oye, oye. Callete, callete, callete, callete. Listen, listen, listen, listen. Silence, silence, silence, silence. It's true. It's true. It's true. It's true. If one of them forgets to say it, the others look at her in horror. She has failed to support her sisters. She's committed treason. It's like intimating her sister is a liar."

Her description of the Romeros was delicious. It made me laugh.

"And then San Mateo," she went on. "Have you ever spent the night in an Indian pueblo? No, I'm sure, not a boy from Missouri. Well, you would be an honored guest. You would be the cousin of Albert, el Juez Sessions. Carasco, the governor, is our friend. Your Indian bed is very hard, just a rug on the floor, and the room is shut up so tight you can't breathe. And you think you hear strange primitive things during the night, but maybe to hear them you must have Indian blood in you like I do."

She was at her best regaling me with Cousin Albert's third stopping-place, almost at the end of his journey.

"The Banburys are the English ones. They raise sheep and wolfhounds, almost as many hounds as sheep and still bigger. When you sit at dinner, there's a tremendous dog like a lean and hungry lobo sitting on each side of you, watching you eat, and very hungry. You think you better be quick getting the food to your mouth or it will be snatched away. You are in a dobe house with a dobe floor five thousand miles from London, and yet everything is English, the talk, the jokes, the table. They even have an English sheepherder, a wonderful old man with a beard like Moses. Queen Victoria is his saint. He was born on the same day, and to him she's the empress of heaven as well as of India. Even their dress is English. One time my father and I came just at dinner. A Lady Somebody or other was at the table in a low-cut evening dress. When she stood up I found she had tucked it into a man's riding-britches."

It was curious to hear Ellen gibe at the ways of the Banburys as if the English were an incomprehensible race when all the time you knew that her own father had been British to his toes. But that was one of her most delightful characteristics, making fun of her own blood, whether English or Spanish, exaggerating incidents and conversation, spicing her talk with liveliness and charm. Tonight I felt flattered that she did it entirely for me.

I fancied at dinner that all the while Ellen chattered and laughed, Chepa served us with a cruel face. Ellen noticed it at last.

"Chepa. What is it?" she asked.

"Nothing, patrona," the servant said.

Ellen's eyes grew thoughtful.

"There is something."

"Nothing, nothing, patrona," Chepa blurted and hurried out in the kitchen.

I saw now that Ellen had sobered, the familiar melancholy shadow fallen across her face.

"Will you go down to the courthouse for me, Jud? See if Amado is still there. Tell him I would like to see him. Right away."

It was necessary to go to several restaurants before finding the sheriff. I thought he looked at me gravely and that he exchanged an uneasy look with the deputy who sat across the table. When finally he arrived at the house, his brother was with him. It was not a good sign.

Ellen received them in the wide hall.

"Have you heard from the judge, Amado?" she asked at once.

"No, señora, not yet," the sheriff said.

"Well, have you heard anything about him?"

"No, señora, nothing definite. There is not time." He said it very elaborately, almost profoundly, too profoundly for the meager information conveyed. It was, I thought, also faintly distant, as if already there was a slight change in position or relationship between them.

"Everyone is so strange," Ellen declared. "First Chepa and now you. I am sure you know something, a rumor perhaps. What have you heard?"

The two brothers exchanged masked glances.

"We have a visitor from Baca County, señora, that is all."

"Who is that?"

"Señor Haddon, the deputy sheriff."

"Well, tell me! What did he come for? What did he have to say?"

"He just brought news that the judge was late, señora."

"Well, how late? Did he finally get there?"

"We don't know, señora. He told us there is no emergency. Court is being postponed till the judge comes. They have a small calendar and plenty of time. No harm is done."

"But where is the judge? Why didn't he get there? Why don't you go out with your men and see where he is?"

"Señor Haddon just got here this afternoon, señora. There has not been time. If you wish, we will go over the trail in the morning. But I am sure it is not necessary, señora. The judge is probably there by this time. Maybe he got sick or his team broke down. You must not worry. If anything had happened, we would have heard about it and Señor Haddon would have found out about it on the way."

The sheriff and his party left in the morning, but learned nothing, except that Cousin Albert had never reached Porvenir. The story of the judge's delay, his unknown whereabouts, and finally his complete disappearance became the chief topic in Moro and the rest of the territory as well. Mama Grande heard of it at the ranch and sent Fidel for particulars. A succession of friends called at the house to ask for news and pay their sympathy. Tom Dold and Dr. Gammel were the faithful ones. Every day they were with Ellen at one time or another. Now that the initial bad news was broken, the Martínez brothers called regularly to report whenever they were in town.

It seemed incredible to me that posses of keen and experienced men from two counties could search the trail and find nothing. They learned that the judge and Willy had spent the first night with the Romeros and the second at the San Mateo pueblo. Next morning an Indian boy shepherd with a small flock of sheep and goats had seen the judge and Willy drive by some eight or ten miles west of the pueblo. The judge had waved to him. Apparently this boy was the last to have laid eyes on either one. They had never reached the Banburys', and none of the Banbury shepherds had seen a trace of them. It was as if they had been swallowed up by the earth itself.

Of all the mysteries that ever gripped the territory, this, I think, has puzzled many of us the most. There had been tragic disappearances in New Mexico before, and a number have happened since, unsolved cases of men and women who set out on a journey through the sparsely settled country never to be seen or heard of again. But most of these concerned obscure people. This had happened to a United States judge on official rounds of duty and to his eleven-year-old son, and yet nothing more could apparently be done about it than if the victims had been nameless emigrants from a passing wagon train.

It was hard on me, but Ellen was the one on whom everything centered. The suspense day after day and night after night must have been very great. Afternoons and evenings she had to receive callers and hear their questions together with the recitation of all the wild stories and rumors going the rounds. One account was that the judge, Willy, and the two horses had been shot and buried along with the burned and dismantled buggy in the sand, and that unless the winds someday might unearth them, their remains would never be found. Another was that Willy had been spared and taken to the lonely highlands of Old Mexico, where he was given to a remote Mexican family to raise so that in time he would no longer remember his mother and father or his New Mexican home. A third story was that Cousin Albert had fled with another woman and taken Willy forcibly along, and that he had died of homesickness and sorrow, to be buried in California.

What turned out worse than the ugly rumors as time went on were the clues that aroused hope only to be proved false. Some claimed they had seen a white boy among the Navajos north of Gallup and that it had been Willy. Some swore the judge had been recognized alive and well, in Denver or El Paso or some other place, that he had seemed dazed as if bereft of his memory. Cousin Albert's horses, Choppo and Dan, were said to have been seen and identified in the hands of strangers, and his pole buggy as well.

Through it all Ellen bore up splendidly, her cheeks a little feverish, her eyes too brilliant perhaps. Sometimes I thought that she bore up too well, that she almost enjoyed the excitement, the attention, the stream of visitors, especially the constant consolation of Tom Dold and Dr. Gammel. She must feel some responsibility, I thought. And yet, here she was, affected certainly but going on almost as before, still the lady, in the last extremity untouchable, the possessor of some quality difficult to name. You could see and hear it and yet never know exactly what it was except that in sorrow, as in pleasure, she was just a little beyond reach, not wholly duty-bound, answerable only to herself.

Then I learned that I was mistaken. The word came that the county authorities had given up the search. Amado Martínez himself broke the bad news one sunny afternoon. He had evidently braced himself for the task, and had asked Mr. Kidd, as a friend of Ellen's, to come along.

"We have done all we can, señora," the sheriff said. "I can't ask the men to keep on looking forever. The country is too big and we have found nothing. Now we must stop."

"That doesn't mean they won't be found sometime, Ellen," Mr. Kidd added kindly. "Why don't you go away for a while? To Denver or St. Louis or some new place where you can forget. Try not to think of Albert and Willy. I'm sure they would want it that way."

This time Ellen didn't go to the door with them when they left. She sat in her chair, very pale. Her face had a transparent quality sometimes seen in the cheeks of the dead, of flesh very transient and about to vanish.

"God forgive me," I heard her say in Spanish, "that I've never been able to cry."

I don't think she knew I was there, or cared. Ever since the dinner when the bad news had come, she

had been strange to me, almost ignored me. I grew
to suspect that she begrudged my being alive and
well, sleeping in Willy's room and going to his
school while he had suffered this unspeakable ca-
lamity.

But now she turned and saw me. Something in
her eyes seized on me. I thought afterward that what
caught her was my kinship to Cousin Albert and
Willy, that I was blood of their blood, the closest
living thing to either of them she had left.

"Never let anyone stop you, Jud, from doing
what you think you should do," she told me passion-
ately. "Had I followed my senses, I would have gone
with Albert, no matter how much he hated to hide
behind my skirts. If he wouldn't have taken me in
his buggy, I could have gone in my own. It might
have shamed him. He might have taken some wild
out-of-the-way trail where no one would see him. But
I could have taken that trail, too. Then if anything
would have happened, I'd have been with him. If the
Jeffcoats jumped him, I'd have been there to talk
them out of it. If in the end they killed him, they
would have had to kill me, too."

At her words the old admiration, affection, and
loyalty for her flooded up in me, and more than
once during the night when I remembered what she
said, warm tears rose to my young eyes.

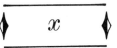

WHEN the authorities gave up, that was when Ellen said she herself would start looking for Cousin Albert and Willy. Tom Dold and Dr. Gammel protested, and Mr. Kidd, when he heard about it, was much disturbed. With Mrs. Kidd he came to the house to advise and urge against it. Ellen heard them all quietly.

"No one will hurt a woman," she said. "Besides, I am taking Fidel and Teofilo along. And Jud," she added with a glance at me. "If he is not afraid."

"Few of us were afraid, Ellen, that they would

dare touch the judge and Willy!" Mr. Kidd reminded.

"Albert never carried a gun," she answered. "I am going armed." Something in her eyes and the way she said it brought up the old uncertainties about her in my mind.

We left for the ranch next morning. Mama Grande heard the plan with her expressionless black eyes.

"If it will help you to go, you must go," she said to Ellen. "But why take another boy into that bad country? What can he do?"

"Jud is Willy's cousin," she reminded. "He missed the first trip. Now he can see where Willy went."

That's what Ellen said, but I felt she had another and deeper reason for taking me, one rather of fate and of meetness. Whatever happened to Cousin Albert she was willing to have happen to her, and what happened to Willy I was not above having happen to me.

We left the ranch in a brilliant sunrise which back in Missouri would have meant rain but here betokened nothing but another Southwestern day. Ellen and I drove in her familiar yellow-top buggy, an object that would betray her identity wherever we went and as far as the moving object could be seen. Critter was in the shafts. Fidel and Teofilo followed in the light wagon. Fidel used it at times to service the sheepherders. Now it was packed to the sheet with provisions, utensils, and bedding, also several saddles. Spare horses and Willy's blue pony, Mono, were on behind.

It was good to look around and see the wagon following us, and especially the presence of Fidel and Teo, the latter the ablest of sheepherders, a good cook and substitute caporal. Both men had inherited the best qualities of both the Spaniard and Indian. I never knew them to be tired. Their eyes, black, sharp, shrewd, fearless, missed nothing. They were, I felt, the ablest of companions in this rough and dangerous country they knew so well. Neither wore guns as the cowboys did, but I was aware that Ellen had had them put firearms in the wagon. Her own light rifle protruded from under the buggy seat on the floor between us.

Ellen said she meant to follow Cousin Albert's route as faithfully as she knew how. Late that afternoon we passed through Cienega Canyon and stayed with the Romeros. The four sisters greeted Ellen like a cousin, a rich, important, and respected cousin toward whom they felt fervid sympathy. Ah, true enough, it was just three—or was it four? —weeks ago that the judge had stopped with them, and Guillermo. Never had they seen His Honor looking more handsome or Guillermo happier. Who then would have supposed that this unknown and terrible evil was waiting for them beyond?

Not until I heard them did I remember what Ellen had told me, how they all repeated what the other said. The air was filled with ojalá, ojalá, ojalá, ojalá, and que lástima, que lástima, que lástima, que lástima and ah dolor, ah dolor, ah dolor, ah dolor till my head swam in the ranch house sala and I escaped to Fidel and Teo by their fire near the corrals, where they were surrounded admiringly by the Romero ranch help. Here men were in control and the talk in keeping with the serious mission.

I was glad to get away in the morning and I think Ellen was, too.

"I hoped they'd remember something important Albert had said," Ellen told me. "Some word about home or that he had changed his plans. But they could tell us nothing. Nothing but por Dios, por Dios, por Dios, por Dios, and es verdad, es verdad, es verdad, es verdad."

She mimicked them to perfection, but there was no fun in it today, only a frightening quality I could not quite name. It was in her eyes, too, as she kept looking ahead. We had left the plains now for higher ground. This beautiful Indian country, I knew, must have been one of the last things Willy and Cousin Albert had seen. But there was little pleasure for us in the cinnamon boles of the giant pines, the patches of sun and shadow, the clear spring-fed mountain streams so precious in a dry land. Then we went down into a deep red rock canyon where we found the irrigated fields and adobe houses of San Mateo pueblo. Here Willy and Cousin Albert had spent their last known night.

The short stout pueblo governor, Carasco, a striking figure in iron-gray hair against a rich copper face and a bright red headband, welcomed us with dignity. Nothing could be hurried. Certain rites of respect and hospitality had to be carried out as if all were well. That evening in his own house, watched by the black eyes of his wife and others, he talked to Ellen about Cousin Albert. He spoke Spanish with a curious Indian accent, hard for me to understand.

I had the impression that he chose his words carefully.

"Who knows what happened to my friend, the white alcalde and his son? There are devils that rise out of the ground. They float through the air and hover over their prey. Sometimes they even ride horses and lie in wait," he added significantly,

watching her closely to see if she caught what he
was saying.

"Yes, I understand, Carasco," Ellen said.

His beady eyes gazed on her with satisfaction.
Then he went on.

"They say the alcalde and his son stay with us at
San Mateo and then are never seen again except by
an Indian boy of the pueblo. It makes it look bad
for the Indian. But the Indians are not devils without reason, señora. Neither the San Mateos or the
Navajos. And if they want to be devils, it would
hardly be to their friend Alberto, but to those who
run their cattle over Indian lands, who take the Indian grass and treat him like dirt when he asks
them to go back to their own country."

His short thick figure mounted on a black horse,
he rode out beside the buggy next morning. Some
three or four miles west of the pueblo, he pointed out
where the Indian sheepherder boy had seen Cousin
Albert's black buggy pass. We were out of the pines
now, in a broad semi-arid country of low cedars.
The wind was blowing, the fine sand already rising.
The gray air and dust-shrouded sky gave everything a look of desolation.

"This is the place, Fidel," Ellen said. "From
here on."

I knew what Ellen meant. I could feel it myself,

a forsaken quality that reminded me of the wind-
swept cemetery at Rancho Zelandia. But here there
was more than human graves abandoned to the
barren waste. Something else could be felt, a wild-
ness far back in time and the human heart, so that
the friendly pueblo Indian waving from his horse
where we had left him seemed like the last outpost
of civilization behind us.

Presently Ellen stopped Critter and motioned
Fidel to drive abreast. They conferred, and from
here on either Fidel or Teo went on foot ahead of the
buggy, eyes keenly examining the trail and ground
adjoining. Sometimes one would leap on a saddled
horse and ride him to the right or left to investigate
some peculiar landmark or shape of sand. The
broken hills were so dry they could support only
scattered cedars, but twice we came to wide draws
or cañadas where flats of green grass and once
grazing cattle testified to the presence of water.
The cattle testified also to something else. We were
now in the country of the Jeffcoats. The hair at the
back of my neck stirred. But whatever Ellen and the
two Mexicans felt was not confided to me.

I saw that our slow careful pace would leave us
far short of any habitation that night. Toward late
afternoon we came to the malpai. We saw it a long
way off, a black ridge of broken blocks of lava

reaching across the face of the land. On one side
the winds had created a region of sand and sand
dunes several miles deep and running as far as the
eye could see. Nothing but salt bushes and blue
sage grew here. This was where Fidel and Teo
showed the greatest interest, examining the ground
minutely, tramping and riding far to investigate
when I could see nothing unusual. With the malpai
still before us, we camped in a draw where a slender
rivulet of water ran clear as crystal from the ugly
black rock. That night, so far as I could tell, Ellen
slept calmly in her sugan. Whenever I roused, which
was often, I saw that one of the Mexicans remained awake, either sitting by the fire, staring into
it in a manner of the sheepherder, or standing off
in the shadows listening. One time it would be
Fidel, another time Teo. I never found out when
they changed.

The men confided little to me. They spoke guard-
edly even to Ellen, but that we stayed there for
several days told volumes. Where the long arm of
malpai finally ended and the trail ran around it
was the place where Fidel and Teo spent the most
time, going over it minutely, examining every yard
of trailside, digging into hundreds of dunes and
spreading the sand out on the ground. In the end
they found nothing.

More than once I grew tired and rode my pony off into the rugged country, hoping to find a clue to the missing travelers in some hidden draw or rincón, yet fearing to catch a glimpse of a Jeffcoat rider watching like an Indian from one of the ridges. But I saw no one and nothing, only the immense dry broken earth, the endless sand and the black landmark of malpai which made it impossible for me to get lost. Beyond lay a wilderness of arroyos, buttes, and mesas, and standing up over them, Gorezón, a natural monument like a giant head and shoulders of a desert tribal god which Willy must have seen from the buggy.

It seemed impossible for any place to be so empty of life, so devoid of human traces. Suddenly I would see a small cloud of dust moving toward me from far away. The feeling that a rider, a human being on a horse, was at last peopling the solitude and coming toward me rose uncontrollably in my breast. Then the small cloud of dust would veer and I could see it was only the wind, after which everything was more lonely and desolate than before. Sometimes, sitting motionless on my horse, I would hear a sound like someone coming, perhaps Willy or Cousin Albert, I thought, riding through the salt bushes behind me. I would whirl and nothing would be there, but in a moment a gust of wind would

reach me and I knew it was again only the mocking
invisible air.

On the side hills, in the small canyons the sand
was eternally blowing, drifting like gray snow close
to the earth. When at last I'd ride back to the malpai I'd see where the tracks of the horses, including
my own, had already filled up and looked like the
rest of the bleak landscape so that the spot where
another person and I had spoken together, a place
touched with human presence and emotion, had become no more than the rest of the deadened landscape.

Each day at the malpai I thought Ellen's face
grew more weary and baffled. Not even the two
nights we stayed at the Banburys' were able to
soften it, the friendliness of the wolfhounds, the
English hospitality, the majesty of the old Lancas-
tershire shepherd, as Ellen had said, like a vision
of Moses in his white beard and hair. This was the
first time, I think, that she ever admitted to herself the possibility that the enigma, like many others
she knew, might never be solved, Cousin Albert and
Willy never found, their fate swallowed up like the
riddle of the Sphinx in the well-kept secrets of this
aloof and silent land.

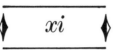

xi

It was strange to come back to Moro without Cousin Albert and Willy, without a trace of them, to know no more about them than before. The town seemed an empty shell today. When we came to La Placita, Ellen stood for a moment at the door as if she couldn't bear entering the dead house. Then she gave a little movement as if she must somehow go through with it, and went in.

What gave me the strangest feeling was passing the courthouse. Cousin Albert had always seemed such a prominent and indispensable figure. It seemed impossible that the county could get along without him. Now already a new man, Judge Saxton, had been appointed from Washington and was at this moment in Porvenir sitting at the spring term of Baca County court where Cousin Albert was to have been.

The worst was to think of Cousin Albert and Willy gone, perhaps done away with, their bodies hidden in some unmarked grave, and then to see Snell Beasley going about his business unaffected, more alive and prosperous than ever. His political power, they said, had risen with Cousin Albert out of the way. Judge Saxton, we knew, was Beasley's friend and had been appointed through his influence. I watched Beasley pass the house on his way to his office in the morning, short, thick, vigorous, and I wondered at the animal sources of such vitality, as I had once wondered in the cedars at the Herculean powers of a sheep-killing bear.

Even Tom Dold, I thought, seemed impressed by Beasley's growing importance. He told Ellen that her brother-in-law had taken a younger man into his office, George Steffy, a lawyer from Baca County. Apparently it gave Beasley more time for outside activities. More than once I saw him drive out in a new rubber-tired topless buggy, the kind we called a runabout. He seemed to be cogitating, scheming as he drove, a heavy figure that caused the springs to sag on the driver's side.

But I think Ellen was unprepared as I was for the news Tom brought her from Beasley one evening at dinner. Carefully, I noticed, he wove Snell Beasley's name into the table talk until Ellen flushed.

"Tom, it seems each time you come you have something good to say about Snell. Perhaps I should be interested in my brother-in-law, but I am not. Please, let's not talk about Snell Beasley."

Tom looked grave.

"This time I've been asked to speak for him, Ellen. He wants me to argue the case in his behalf."

"Argue what case?"

"Your willingness to sell Critter."

Ellen went white.

"I wouldn't dream of parting with Critter, Tom. And if I did, hardly would I put him at the mercy of that brute."

"I was only interested," Tom went on gravely, "in the possible mending of relations between you two. It might also change things between you and your sister."

I could see that Ellen was angry.

"I am not interested in any change of relations

between Snell Beasley and me, Tom. Between Ana and me, yes. But I don't see that giving him Critter would help that."

Through the rest of dinner I saw that Ellen looked at him with intense questioning eyes. What she thought she did not tell me, but I suspect she kept learning, as I had, the bitter truth that Cousin Albert was indeed gone, that another power reigned and even Tom was ready to bow before it. The king was dead, long live the king. The phrase ran through my head that night. I had never quite understood it before.

But if Beasley was king now, at least he couldn't have Critter. It was a small thing, I knew, beside the loss of Willy and Cousin Albert. Nevertheless, it gave me satisfaction. We still had the fastest horse in the territory, or so I thought. I wasn't so sure of it when we heard that Beasley had bought a racing horse in Texas and was bringing him home to use in the shafts of his runabout.

I asked Manuel about it the day the horse was led down the alley to the stable next door, followed by a small crowd. Manuel regarded me with black unreadable eyes.

"Pretty fine-looking nag. Hardly six years old. About ten hundred pounds. I can chin fifteen hands, but I couldn't chin him. Looks fast. Arabian blood,

Goyo told me. Day after tomorrow, he says, they take him down and exercise him on the track."

The Moro track was an open piece of dry sandy land on the other side of the railroad. There was a half-mile circular course and a straightaway on one side for quarter racing. I went there on Saturday afternoon and was surprised to see that a few other persons had gathered. One prominent man of town arrived in his own rig to watch. Beasley's new horse was already there, and my heart sank as I saw him on the track. He was a thoroughbred, a little longer and rangier than Critter, a chestnut and more handsome, with a lighter, almost blond mane and tail. Moreover, he was younger than Critter, just coming into his power, while Critter was soon to pass the peak of his prime, if already he hadn't done so. Looking at him, I could well believe what they said about his Arabian blood. His speed was impressive, and there was a professional look about him in the sulky with Goyo on the seat, his legs spread. Several men I knew held their watches òn him and afterward spoke jovially to Beasley, who had stood alone, his thick neck thrust forward, watching the performance.

There was a great deal of talk in Moro about the new horse that month, occasional brief accounts in the *Optic* of small races in which Beasley's horse

left the others far behind. The *Optic* called him the
Racer. Most Anglos referred to him as the Arabian,
the Mexicans as El Arabe. Beasley challenged any
horse in the territory, and this was freely quoted in
talk and print. But if Ellen saw or heard of it, she
ignored it. The only time she referred to it was
when, nettled by her silence to the challenge, I
blurted out that people thought she was afraid of
running Critter.

I knew then by the instant brilliance of her eyes
that I had struck fire.

"You haven't been down to the track, Jud?"

I kept silent. She gazed at me with that Spanish
look of feminine hurt. Then she went on.

"Jud, when a member of Mama Grande's people
died, they believed in mourning. A black cloth was
put up at the door to tell people that those in the
house were in sorrow so no one going by would laugh
too loud or carry on unseemly. The native people
respected it. Most of the men took off their hats
when they passed. If the person who died was near
and dear to us, the black cloth was kept up till it
literally wore to pieces or blew away. Sometimes it
was up for two years."

She stopped and watched me to see how I was taking it. Then she went on.

"The Anglos, when they came, had other customs.

Now, I am part Anglo. I'm of the newer generation.
I hate mourning. I refuse to put it on when I don't
know what happened to Albert and Willy, where
they are, whether they are living or dead. But that
doesn't mean I race horses or even talk about racing
them. I hoped that since Willy and Albert were
your cousins, you'd feel the same way, that you
wouldn't go near the track. People may see you and
think that I sent you to spy on Snell's new horse.
We know this is untrue, but they don't. The truth
is that even if Albert and Willy were still here, I
wouldn't race Critter. Critter isn't a racehorse. He's
my buggy horse. He's devoted to me and I'm devoted to him. Long before Albert and Willy left
us, people urged me to put him on the track. But
I never have and I never will. I think this should be
made more emphatic. The next time Tom comes to
the house, I'll ask him to inform Snell and who
ever else is necessary."

From the way Lawyer Beasley went by the next
time I saw him, I suspected that Tom had told him.
He had a look on his face that might be described
as curdled amusement. He seemed to take Ellen's
refusal as a kind of joke, as if he were saying to himself, so you think you won't race with me? It was
curious to see an emotion like that working in the
thick flesh and face of the man. He seemed to bal-

ance his heavy form with a certain triumph as if he felt she was afraid and that everyone else knew it, too, which gave him the title by point of rules.

But I didn't know Snell Beasley very well then, nor the extremes of cunning to which his ambition went, that he never would be satisfied with victory by forfeit, that his amusement and sense of triumph came rather from something else he was working out in his mind.

It was true that Ellen had put on no mourning. On the other hand, she had certainly given no parties since Cousin Albert had left, and when she went to another house for the evening it was only for a quiet dinner with friends. Mostly she busied herself with the ranch, was out with Mama Grande half the time. Once when Dr. Gammel called and found her away, he told me it was a good thing she had the sheep business to throw herself into. It took her mind off her tragedy.

Inevitably, when she was in town, she drove out for a ride in the afternoon. Often she took me along, and I could feel the good it did her when we got away from the lonely house and still more when we reached the end of town. Here were scenes with which Cousin Albert or Willy had been less actively associated and from which they did not keep leaping into her mind. Also, I think it helped her just to go, to keep moving, to have the wheels turning and Critter bearing her on.

This afternoon she was not at the house when I came home. I went out to the stable. Critter's box stall was empty. Manuel told me she had left two hours before, that she said something about driving north to the Saturnino Montoyas'. As we talked we saw Goyo take the Beasley horse down the alley from the stable next door.

"Now where is he going in the runabout this time of day?" Manuel rumbled, moving to the door and looking after. "It's late for his patrón to drive anyplace."

Something in what he said or the way he said it aroused my curiosity, and I followed. As I went down the alley I fancied an air of expectancy in Old Town. A few more people than usual were out in the plaza, most of them moving down toward Audiencia Street. They glanced at me curiously, I thought, as I came after, some with amusement, some with anticipation in the dark eyes. I found the racehorse and runabout had stopped in front of Beasley's office. A little group gathered around them. As I approached, Beasley himself came out. I couldn't hear his careful orders to Goyo, who started driving the racehorse away. Beasley looked around, pleased, at the crowd. Tom Dold and Frank

Gomez, the county treasurer, were across the street
in front of the courthouse.

"If she won't race that fast horse of hers on the
track, we'll have to do it on her own ground," he
called.

I learned afterward that Beasley himself had
seen Ellen drive north on New Town Road. It was
the same road my father had taken to the Greenhorns and Ellen to the Pereas'. But all I was aware
of at the time was people moving down Audiencia
Street. I followed, giving no sign of recognition to
Tom Dold, and I noticed that he gave none to me.

A few spectators already waited on New Town
Road when we reached it, and the number increased
as the news got abroad. The hack that customarily
met the train came with some citizens from New
Town. They piled out, hailing friends in the crowd.
A spirited air pervaded most of the spectators,
Anglos and Mexicans alike. But uneasiness, I
thought, could be felt among the sheep people, and
this was my own feeling.

Far up the road I could see Goyo driving slowly
north. Not a sign of another horse or rig as far as
my eyes could reach. Maybe she won't come, I said
to myself hopefully, surprised at my reluctance to
have the match finally come off, I who had earlier
urged her to arrange it. Finally, far up the road

toward the Montoyas' I thought I saw a puff of dust
rising.

Before I could be sure, Lino García came along
with his old crowbait and water cart loaded with
barrels and boys. They stopped and Pas Ramírez
sent a García boy back among the empty barrels to
make room for me on the seat. Then we drove north
on the road to see what we could see. The dust now
included a dot, and my eyes strained on the speck,
hoping it might be only a light wagon or saddle
horse of some rancher.

Pas Ramírez was the first to identify it.

"It's her—la doña," he said, adding the latter
out of respect to me.

I couldn't be sure, but as we went on and the
speck came toward us, my eyes finally made out the
yellow-top buggy. I knew the horse must be Critter, probably trotting a little faster on the way
home. Alone in the seat would be Ellen, unsuspect-
ing what lay ahead. As she approached we saw
Goyo, still traveling toward her, look over his shoulder several times as if measuring the distance back
to Old Town. He drew the racer to a walk as the
yellow-top buggy came close.

Hardly had the two rigs passed when Goyo
swung the chestnut around. It seemed Beasley had
given him wise and wily instructions, for he waited

until the buggy must have been a hundred yards in front. Then we thought we saw him shake the reins and the racehorse started to come from behind. We were not close enough to see, but I could imagine Critter's ears pricking at the sound of hoofs overtaking him and Ellen tightening the reins to hold him, which I knew well she could never do. All we definitely saw was Goyo pulling out to the left to go around, and then the two horses side by side and neither one passing, by which we knew they had started to run.

"Mira! Here they come!" Pas Ramírez yelled, and we all stood up.

Those were the days of no fences. The road lay across the prairie and was wide as you chose to make it. My mind was taken up, as always when I came in contact with Beasley, with the astute craftiness of the schemer. Here was a natural racecourse, a straightaway for miles, as were so many Western roads, with Old Town, including its audience of inhabitants, as the finish. Looking at the horses from in front, we had no idea how fast they were already coming. Only in the nick of time did Lino recognize our danger. Never, in my opinion, would either of the two horses have stopped for us. Lino got his cart off the road just as they went by. I had a glimpse of Critter, the bit between his teeth, that

stubborn forward look to his head and neck, and of
Ellen looking helpless and exasperated in the
buggy, sawing vainly on the lines to hold him, while
half a length behind him the racehorse tore on, eyes
glazing, his mane and tail streaming, Goyo half
raised from the seat, the whip in his hand.

Once they were by, all we could see were the two
rigs through a cloud of dust. Although Lino
whipped his crowbait and sent him galloping behind them, none of us could tell for sure which was
ahead, only that they were still on opposite sides
of the road as they reached Old Town. By the time
we got there, they were far beyond. I had a glimpse
of Tom Dold and the county treasurer looking
thoughtful and of Beasley turning away darkly
toward his office while the Mexicans chattered in
great animation and the sheepmen looked solidly
pleased.

We learned afterward that never for a moment
had Goyo been able to get around the yellow-top
buggy, that at the outskirts of town Ellen was almost a length ahead, and that when they reached
where the crowd stood the thickest, Critter was still
going like such a torrent she daren't think of turning up Audiencia Street but kept him on New Town
Road. He was halfway to the railroad tracks before
she could stop him. The water cart took me part of

the distance. I got out and ran the rest on foot. When I reached the buggy, Ellen, white and shaken, was driving Critter slowly back, his coat laid from neck and shoulders halfway to his rump with sweat.

"You devil!" she was saying angrily to him when she stopped to let me in.

"He was wonderful," I told her.

"He's a stubborn, vain, unprincipled brute!" she answered. "I could kill him with good grace."

We saw a black knot of people up around Audiencia Street waiting for her to drive back, but to my disappointment she turned up Alameda Street to the plaza to avoid them. I protested.

"They saw Critter come in ahead and that's enough," she insisted. "They shouldn't have seen that much. There was no occasion for a race at this time and no decency in it. They should know it."

xii

DESPITE Ellen's anger over the race, it did her good, I think. Her victory over Beasley softened, if faintly, some of her bitterness against him. She felt more resigned. By the time fall came around, it seemed that the agitation over Cousin Albert's and Willy's disappearance had begun to blow over. Then word arrived that a sheepherder in a remote corner of Baca County had seen a cowboy from the Bar B ranch riding Dan, one of Cousin Albert's horses. Salomón Baca, owner of the sheep, had taken his herder to town to swear out an affidavit.

A few nights later the herder's flock was scattered
and trampled by horses and the herder himself
killed. A warrant had been issued for the cowboy
and Beasley had been engaged to defend him.

Now things were all stirred up again. The incident, with many versions and details, was on everyone's lips, reviving the earlier tragedy that had
mothered it. Hardly had all this happened when
word came that a body had been discovered. That
evening Amado Martínez called at the house and
was closeted with Ellen. They wouldn't let me in
the room. When the sheriff left, he patted my
shoulder. Ellen had come out more composed than
I expected.

"I have news for you, Jud. They've found your
father," she said.

It's always been very much of a riddle to me the
way things happen, the pattern in which they appear. We expect one thing, foresee a certain con-
clusion, but something unforeseen often comes
about. It's as if the mind or power making the moves
on life's chessboard plays the game on a scale and
with a code that we can never comprehend. Try as
we might to take in all the facts and sift the proba-
bilities, what eventually turns out is often something that none of us expected. Here had been the
tragic disappearance of one of the most prominent

persons in the territory and his son, a mystery which many had tried to solve. It was generally supposed they had been buried in the desolate wastes, and now a body was found. But instead of it being one of the missing pair, it was the body of my father, whose disappearance by this time had been almost forgotten except by me and I had stoutly believed him still alive.

When Ellen told me, my face must have gone white, for she led me to one of the couches and put her arm around me. She told me quietly all the sheriff had said to her. The body had been found in a high canyon in the Greenhorn Mountains, where it had lain covered by snow most of the year. Apparently he had been taken there alive, murdered, and the money stolen. They were bringing the body back to Moro now.

"Don't worry. Your father will have Christian burial in the Protestant cemetery. I'll see Reverend Crandall myself in the morning."

We found next day that the sheriff hadn't told everything, that much of the body had been preyed on by birds and vermin and only the pair of heavy trousers had kept the flesh intact below. They wouldn't let me see it, but I think Ellen had and it must have made a shocking impression on her. All the while the minister read the burial service over the tightly closed pine coffin, her mind, I think, was not on the ravages of wild creatures and the elements on the body inside of it, but on the bodies of Cousin Albert and Willy, still unfound.

There were those who said that Ellen Sessions had refused to wear mourning for her husband and son but had put it on for the father of her cousin by marriage. This was unadulterated nonsense. My father's death and burial had only brought home to her the shocking realities of Willy's and Cousin Albert's disappearance. Now she felt she had no other way than to accept them as dead and all it implied. She wore no mourning at my father's funeral. The day afterward she took the train to Denver to buy materials, and, when she came back, called the dressmakers in.

She looked older, thinner, and if anything more beautiful in black the morning she asked me to stay home from school. Her face, I thought, was like marble.

"I want to call on Mr. Beasley," she told me. She had never called him that before. "I haven't discussed the matter with Tom or anyone, but I feel I would like to have a witness. You're the only son I have now, Jud, and I wish you would go along." Just the way she looked at me, I felt a dependence that made me more of a man.

Never have I fancied lawyers' offices very much in general or Snell Beasley's in particular. Much would I have given to get out of going with her that morning. I put on my best gray suit and new black stockings as if dressing for church or the scaffold, and Ellen, when I saw her, did not reassure me. She seemed calm enough, as if going to church, but there was with it a certain sad and bitter dedication which I have seen some women assume in religious services but which Ellen had never before affected.

To my surprise, Manuel was waiting with Critter and the buggy outside. We could have easily walked the short distance to the plaza, then crossed it to Audiencia Street and down half a block to Burro Alley and the dusty brick building across the street from the courthouse.

More than once had Ellen instructed Willy and me how, when we were with her, to leap out first and help her down from the buggy. I tried to do that now, especially since there were men in front of the courthouse watching. I'm sure I didn't know what I was doing, but Ellen gravely accepted my help. Then, without knocking, she went into the office and I followed.

My first impression was the strong stale scent of tobacco and tobacco ashes and the stronger reek of cuspidors. I saw George Steffy look up in surprise and a little fright, I thought, from his desk piled with books and papers, while behind him through the parted doors which did not open on hinges as other doors I knew but were drawn apart, I had a glimpse of a deeper and more dangerous region. This Ellen at once entered, not stopping at Mr. Steffy's desk to inquire as I supposed she would.

There was nothing for me to do except push after. I found we were in a large room with shelves. One whole wall was lined with yellow leather books, and on the other hung framed pictures of men and of horses, of the Beasley house, of the courthouse, and even of the corner of Burro Alley and Audiencia Street with Beasley standing in front of his brick office. There were chairs and a green bag on the floor, and in the corner the largest desk I ever saw, a great flat-top piled still more with documents and books than George Steffy's, and behind the desk the thick form and powerful face of Willy's Uncle Snell. His face wasn't lifted. It was only the eyes that peered up, almost squinted, as if to say, who is this?—the fierce large eye and the smaller drooping one which I had heard referred to as "his little bitty eye." I don't know which one frightened me the most.

Hearing something, I turned and saw George

Steffy hastily take his hat and leave, closing both doors carefully behind him. I had the feeling that Beasley would dress him down properly afterward for not stopping us, but now that he was cornered and had no way to escape except with ignominy, he faced us and I felt that in the last analysis it was not he who was cornered but we who had foolishly entered his den and put ourselves at his mercy.

Even Ellen seemed aware of this. She seated herself on the edge of a chair with a rawhide seat which looked dirty to me, and regarded him for a few moments.

"I've come to you in peace, Snell, to ask a favor."

She said it humbly, almost abased, but I saw it didn't appease her brother-in-law. At her words a tongue of red fire seemed to leap up and enliven the cavern of his fierce eye for a moment while his little bitty eye gave no clue. She went on.

"I want to ask if you will speak to your clients for me. I mean the cattlemen in Baca County. I beg of them to tell me something. Oh, I don't want to know who was involved in this terrible thing or any detail of what happened. All I ask of them is to let me know where the bodies of Willy and Albert may be found so I can bring them to Moro, have them decently buried and the Christian service read over them."

It seemed a small and deserving request to me, but I noticed no answering pity or sympathy in his eyes.

"And you feel my cattlemen clients should be able to tell you that?" he asked in a tone which I didn't recognize then but which I do now as that of a powerful lawyer leading a witness into a trap where he would presently destroy him.

"I do," Ellen answered.

"Perhaps you feel that I myself might be able to tell you?"

"God forbid," Ellen said so low I could scarcely hear her.

"What do you mean by that?"

"Just God forbid," she repeated.

To my dismay, an expression of righteous indignation gripped him at her reply. The lower part of his face twitched, and I had the feeling that deeper forces were inexplicably stirring and rising from unknown pits inside of him.

"You say you come in peace and then insult and vilify me by your aspersions." He spoke in a surprisingly calm and controlled voice. "First, let me point out that there is not the slightest proof that your boy and husband are dead as you assume, let alone murdered and hidden in the wilderness as you insinuate. Secondly, you assume that the perpetra-

tors of such a gross and hideous crime are my own
clients who could tell you where the bodies are, if
they wished, and that this makes me either a dupe
ignorant of the true nature of my clients or a
confederate equally guilty with them of murder.
Thirdly, you set up this imaginary set of circumstances and accusations and forget that if these
grossly improbable things were true it would still
be you and your husband who by persecution of
other human beings set in motion acts against God
and man that brought the final culmination to pass."

If he had stopped there, I thought he might have
had something, but his flush of triumph carried him
on. His little bitty eye twinkled like a dark star.

"Finally, you seem to have overlooked or won't
admit the report I have heard from a number of
sources, and which from association and relationship with you I must respect, that Albert has long
been growing weary of your efforts to dominate and
influence his judicial acts, so that finally he had
no other course than to knowingly and willfully
abandon you to your fate."

Ellen rose to her feet.

"That's a lie, Snell, and you know it."

He sat looking at her with satisfaction that was
positively evil.

" 'The truth is mighty and will prevail,' " he

quoted. " 'The mills of God grind slowly but they grind exceedingly small.' For a long time you have been riding high. You have done what you liked and been above the law. You have influenced and manipulated the law in the cases of others, causing in the end the ruin of your brother, your husband and son. You have even tried to interfere with the personal life of your sister and her household. But now reality has caught up to you and you will have to face justice and reformed conditions. No longer are you able to dictate to the bench."

Ellen's cheeks were flat white.

"Are you going to get me the information I asked, Snell, so Albert's and Willy's bodies can be brought home and decently buried?"

He gazed at her with baneful delight.

"I have told you that I know nothing, that my clients know nothing. Now I will add that, on the contrary, did my clients know something and had they given me the information in the priestly confidence that exists between an honorable lawyer and his client, I could and would tell you nothing, and the courts would sustain me. No, not even if the bodies of Albert and Willy were buried as you say, their remains to be dug up by coyotes and other scavengers of the wild and never to be found or seen by humankind again."

He was a devil, the very devil himself, I thought.
For a little while Ellen stood shocked and trembling.
Then she took my arm and we left. Critter and the
yellow-top buggy were waiting. I helped her in. We
drove off. She said no word to me on the way home,
not until she reached the door of the house.

"I hoped it could be done without further blood-
shed, Jud, but now I see he must be dealt with as the
dog he is."

"Cousin Ellen, don't!" I begged, following her
into the house, where she stopped and turned.

"What, Jud?" she asked quietly.

"I don't know," I stammered, unwilling to put
my fear into words that could trouble us both.

Her eyes probed mine.

"I'm glad you came along, Jud. It's sometimes
better to know that life may be a more serious and
inescapable thing than you think when you are
young. Then you feel the world is good and troubles
can always be avoided. But when you grow older
you find that they hem you in, first on one side and
then on the other, and finally you get to a point
where you can no longer live honorably, when the
dead cry out for justice but nobody will administer
it and you've got to attend to it yourself."

I didn't know fully what she meant, but I knew
enough. As she disappeared behind the door, I had

a moment's glimpse of her room, the carved bureau and wardrobe, the Brussels carpet on the floor, the polished French brass bed. There were lacy things hanging from the ceiling, and a painted fragile china lamp on a stand. All was very feminine except for one jarring note. In the far corner beside the bed I had the glimpse of an object from the ranch. Only the barrel was visible above the elaborate bed-cover, but it was enough. I knew that ever since Charley had been shot, she had kept a pearl-handled revolver lying on the marble-top table at the head of her bed. Now I was aware that on our return from her search of the malpai she must have brought her light rifle to town, and I wondered how she had managed it in the buggy so that I didn't see it.

Ellen didn't appear for lunch or dinner that day. This was most unusual. Not even on the day the news came about Cousin Albert and Willy had she taken to her room. I hoped that Dr. Gammel or Tom Dold or some of her other friends might come this evening, but no one called.

"How is she?" I asked Chepa when she brought out the tray that evening.

"You can see for yourself," Chepa said, showing me the food almost untouched.

"Shouldn't I go for Dr. Gammel?"

"For what? She is not sick. She is not in bed. She

just walks the room. She is like a leona. I heard where you were today, but what did she do?"

"It was Señor Beasley who did it," I said.

"Ah, him!" Chepa nodded grimly and went out in the kitchen.

That evening I lay on a settee in the wide hall near the door to her room. Twice I heard the scratching of a pen. The cutting strokes made me uneasy. Later when all was silent, I heard the door open.

"Jud, what are you doing there?"

"I guess I lay down and fell asleep."

"Well, go to your bed," she ordered me.

I did with reluctance as she told. There was something about my room this evening that gave me an unpleasant feeling. I looked out of the window. Then I knew what it was. Light shone in the Beasley home next door, especially in the room opposite Ellen's bedroom. I could see just the top of the window. Before the wall had been put up Willy and I had often watched his Uncle Snell sitting in this room, which served as an office at home. Invariably he was at his desk under the light of a green-shaded oil lamp. The same colored light came from the top of the window tonight. Standing on the bed, I could peer over the wall and see him sitting at the desk now, going over a pile of papers.

Ellen's room was next to mine. From the absence

of light falling on our side of the wall, I could tell that it was in darkness. And yet from time to time I thought I heard her moving about. Then I couldn't lie still, but had to stand up on my hard Mexican bed and stare at the black target of Beasley sitting at his desk by the green-shaded lamp. I would stand a long time, rigid, waiting, listening, until from sheer weariness I would lie down again.

Once when I pushed back the covers and stood up, the light from Beasley's window was gone. The brick house was dark, the windows dim and silent. When I lay down, I could see far over the roof next door the stars shining steadily in the velvety dark-blue territorial sky. Gratefully I closed my eyes and let sleep overtake me.

✦ xiii ✦

I SELDOM saw Ellen now until noon. She stayed in
the seclusion of her room. What she did in there
all the morning was a mystery that I felt could be
fathomed only by other ladies and their maids.
Chepa went in from time to time with hot water,
breakfast and other things. Sometimes I would hear
talking, but it was mostly in Chepa's voice or that of
Epifania, who went in, too. When Ellen dressed and
came out at last, I was always a little shocked at
what I saw. This was not the Ellen I knew. She

looked as if she hadn't slept, as if she had had a
battle most of the night.

Nights were bad for me, too. I thought what a
relief it would be to leave the tragic white house and
its brick companion next door. I asked why we
didn't go to the ranch. Out there I felt I could
sleep untroubled by every stir and creaking. It
would be pure bliss to crumple up on my stomach at
night and let the world go, knowing it would take
care of itself till morning. But she wouldn't leave.
Something would come into her face.

"No, Jud, I can't. Not yet," she would say.

Several times when I heard Chepa or Epifania
going in or out or when Dr. Gammel came, I tried
to post myself where I would get a glimpse inside.
I wanted to see if the rifle was still there, but never
was I quick enough.

Tom and the doctor called most every day. I know
Tom Dold asked her to marry him, and I felt that
the doctor had always wanted her. But she was impatient with them both.

"What do you have in your blood that other men
don't have?" she asked me once, and I learned that
she was thinking of Cousin Albert. "Why do some
men talk too much? It's a woman's art and right. A
man should sit quietly and let a woman do the talking. He should be warmed and refreshed by it. And

if the woman is in no mood to talk, he should be sympathetic and silent. But I must listen to Tom Dold reciting all the petty doings of the court, especially of Snell Beasley, and all the stories going the rounds. Half of them he's told me before. Then I must be bored stiff listening to the doctor talk about the mistakes of Moses and the sins of the church and the morality of being an atheist or agnostic and all the sayings of Robert Ingersoll. You know I'm no saint myself or too strong a believer, but I can't swallow the righteousness of the ungodly and the wickedness of the good."

The third of the faithful trio who came to see her was Father Goshard, the big gaunt Belgian, who could often be seen with a small Mexican girl in each hand in front of the church and rectory on the plaza. He liked young people and usually asked me to stay in the sala when he called. Ellen seldom treated him with the pious reverence showed him by most of her people. The first time I heard them together I feared he would be offended, but soon I saw that he took delight in her attitude toward him as an equal and in her quick readiness to give her opinion on the most sacred of matters.

I remember once after they had disputed back and forth for an hour, Ellen turned to me.

"It's not in me to let any man get the upper

hand of me, Jud, not even my saintly and dogmatic spiritual father."

That, I reflected, was a fair statement of Ellen.

"I agree with the French woman, Father, on your silly story about Eve," she said at another time. "Not temptation but gluttony must have been the first sin. I think you'd agree, too, if you priests were women with a babe guzzling and gorging at your breast."

It shocked me a little, but the priest only laughed that day. He seemed heartily to enjoy her unpredictable contradictions. But he did not laugh now at her acrimonious thrusts at God and man, and especially not at her bitterness over the impunity of Snell Beasley.

"Why should he still be alive after what happened to Albert and Willy?" she asked once.

" 'Vengeance is mine, saith the Lord.' "

"Then why are there public trials and executions?" she said quickly. "Why not let it all to God?"

"There is the duty of serving the established courts of law and order," the priest said. "And there is taking the law into our own hands, serving the baser passions in our own breasts."

"I fight," Ellen said in a low voice. "But it goes hard and takes very long."

" 'My yoke is easy and my burden is light!' "
the priest quoted. "You are young. There is still
peace and happiness for you."

"If you refer to another marriage sometime, Father, it could never be even if I wished it," she said.
"I'll never really know if Albert is dead."

The old priest watched her from the deep eyes
in his gaunt face.

"Why don't you submit to the will of God, child?"
he asked. "Where and by what means Judge Sessions and Willy came to leave this life, we don't
know. But the fact of their departure is evident to
all. It's better to accept it and have Masses said for
your son's soul."

"Sometimes it's best not to admit too much to
one's self, Father," Ellen answered. "So long as
there's hope, there's less evil in the world and in the
heart."

I think the priest caught that.

"You put your faith not in God, child, but in
rumors," he chided. "I hear these rumors, too. Somebody has seen the judge or Willy in California
or Wyoming or Old Mexico—mostly in Old Mexico.
They are living or kept there now against their
will. It takes money to investigate these rumors. I
hear someone is always traveling far for you at your
expense."

"What is money beside the lives of those you love?" she asked.

"There are many rumors in the world and little truth in any of them, child. Their only vitality is in the hope they arouse. When they prove false, there is bitter disappointment and renewal of hatred."

"That's true, Father," Ellen admitted. "But if someone tells me he has seen Albert or Willy alive, I can't sit idly by and do nothing. They may need me. And I can't sit idly by when my own brother-in-law defends the man seen with one of Albert's horses and who murdered the sheepherder who testified to it."

"Have no fear, child," the priest said, "God will not defend the wicked. The courts will never acquit him."

That's what we all thought, and it was a shock even to me when word came from Baca County that the cowboy had been freed. The Baca County jury, we heard, had been putty in Beasley's hands. I hoped for his own safety that he would be detained at court in Baca County a long time. But at noon the second day after the news, Manuel told me that the racehorse was back in the stable.

Most of the stables of Old Town were of one-story adobe. Even ours, although larger than most, was of a single floor, with a large carriage room

and another for hay and feed and a still smaller one
with harness on the wall and a bunk for Manuel.
The Beasley stable was different, of brick like the
house and of a shape like stables of rich men in
Missouri, with gables and a fancy roof rising to a
kind of central pinnacle topped with a weathervane
where an iron arrow swung in the wind.

I was standing in the alley looking gloomily at
the brick house and wondering how it would all end
when I saw a hand beckon me from the stable. Walk-
ing closer, I saw it again. The doors were open.
Beasley's runabout and sulky were both there, the
shafts up against the wall, the racer in his stall, but
Goyo was out somewhere. I wondered what I had
seen. Then Felicitas stepped out from behind the
steps as I went in.

"What do you want?" she demanded.

"I don't want anything," I told her.

"You'll catch it, coming over here."

"What did you call me for, then?"

"I never called you."

"Maybe not out loud, but your hand did."

"It did not."

"Then you must have the St. Vitus dance or something."

"I don't have St. Vitus dance, but you'll have it
if my father catches you."

"Maybe he won't be up and around long to catch me," I told her enigmatically.

We fought for a good while, but she didn't tell me to go. The longer I stayed, the surer I was she had beckoned me. When her small brother, Jackie, came in and surprised us, she surprised me by calling me Goyo and making sure Jackie understood by pointing to me.

"Goyo! Goyo!" she said.

"Goyo," little Jackie said too, peering at me doubtfully, and I marveled at the inherited cunning in the girl, protecting herself by preparing his brain if he should repeat anything of my presence to his father.

"Goyo goes by-by now," I said mockingly and turned to leave.

"Wait," she said, swiftly coming after me to the door where she took a small bunch of flowers from under her apron. I don't know the English name, but we called them maritas in Spanish. She held them out to me.

"For Willy," she said in a low voice.

"Willy's dead," I said harshly.

"I know," she told me.

For a moment I considered taking the flowers from her hand and throwing them on the manure pile, but in the end I took them to Ellen, saying they

were for Willy from Felicitas. I refrained from adding what she had said about Willy being dead. For
the first time in days I saw Ellen's face soften. She
poured water herself from her bedroom pitcher and
set the flowers in a vase on the marble-top table in
her room.

◆ *xiv* ◆

IT WAS Felicitas's flowers, I believe, that for a time staved off the inevitable, touched a spot in Ellen that neither Tom nor the doctor or priest had been able to reach. Before the maritas wilted, she dried them and tied the golden-brown bunch with white ribbon. They were the only flowers she had to stand for Willy's death, and they made a bond now between her and Felicitas. But they made, if anything, no more than an uneasy truce between her and Felicitas's father, I felt, and that it would never last.

Gracias á Dios, Chepa used to say, that we mortals never know what is ahead for us. Now I have heard Mexicans speak otherwise, especially old sheep-herders who had spent their lives reading the sky and range. They insist that the future is written down for us, every whit, that there are always signs. Fidel, the wisest man on the ranch, used to answer, yes, of course, it is all written down, but who can read the handwriting of el Dios? As for signs, who knows for sure what they mean until he can look back and see what they portended by the things that came to pass?

What was destined to happen those years is all to be found today in dusty files. First came the heavy winter snowfall that turned the range the following summer into a garden for those sheep that hadn't been smothered by the snow. Then, like the lean years in Egypt after the fat years, came the great drought. For some twenty months no snow or rain worthy of the name fell.

But the worst was not yet, not until after the national elections. I remember going to the depot for Ellen to get the latest returns. Cleveland, if elected, had promised to put wool on the free list. What happened is history, but the interpretation is something else. I have heard it argued endlessly pro and con, depending on which side of the political

fence you stood. Some claimed it was the free wool
that brought the panic of '93, others that it was
the drought. All I know is that wool dropped to
seven cents a pound, in some cases to five, that sheep
sold for a dollar apiece, and that such a time of ruin,
desolation, and wretchedness ensued over the territory as I never saw before or since.

The only good I knew it to do was to bring an
end to Ellen's mourning over what had happened
to Willy and Cousin Albert.

"Thank God they are not living now!" more than
once she told me.

It troubled me to think that it took a terrible
means as this to bring a change in her, to restore
her active old-time self. Energies that had lain
dormant or been dammed up in her so long began
to be released again in their natural channels. I
remember her especially the following spring on the
ranch which by now had become a ghastly place.
The great Johnson y Campo lamb crop, once a rich
source of income, had turned into a cruel liability.
As they were born, lambs had to be killed to save
their mothers. If we didn't, the milkless ewes would
walk off and leave them to starve anyway. But
Ellen was the patrona again, and I can still hear
her voice heartening the discouraged lambers, the

range around them desolate with dust and dead
sheep under a pitiless sky.

The lambing was scarcely over when Mama
Grande died. Fidel showed me the ground at the
bottom of the grave still damp from the snows of
two winters before, but from there on up the brown
Southwestern soil was dry as dust.

"She knew better days. These were hard for her
to take," Ellen told me. "She is better off out of this
kind of world!"

But if Mama Grande was better off, Ellen wasn't.
Just the sight of Beasley, when he arrived, brought
up all I had heard of him lately—that there was no
holding him, that these were times ripe for him and
his kind. He was making himself a great fortune,
perhaps the largest in the territory, calling notes,
foreclosing, buying ranches for little or nothing.
The days of the panic were only harvest time to him.
I remembered what Father Goshard had said, that
no man had great influence unless God gave him the
power, and it sorely tested my faith in religion and
goodness that God could favor and support such a
man as J. Snell Beasley.

He came to the ranch alone driving his racehorse,
which he ordered Teofilo to put up, almost as if he
himself were the patrón. He met Ellen coolly and

without pretense of regret at the death of his children's abuelita.

"Your sister hasn't been too well," he said. "I thought it best if she and the children were spared the ordeal of the funeral and also finding the ranch in such a state."

It was almost as if he had said a state of ruin and decay.

"I'm sorry for Ana's sake that she didn't come. All of us have only one mother," Ellen said.

He gave that cool look of his, a little out of focus, a little amused, a little terrifying, hinting without words or details of things still to come. I watched him at the funeral and afterward, not mingling with the mourners but striding about, putting his nose here and there, asking sharp questions of the peons, inspecting the ranch buildings, finally ordering his horse and buggy and driving off with good-byes to no one.

"He is one I am glad to see go," Teofilo told me. "He makes my stomach to curl. He looks and he looks, but he tells nobody what he sees."

"They say he has the evil eye," an old man said. "Now which is it, the big eye that stares at you like a steer, or the little eye that squints at you like a bull?"

"I do not know about things like the evil eye,"

Fidel answered. "All I know is sorrow that our old doña is gone. Now our young doña stands alone against him and Doña Ana."

In the days that followed I saw, or thought I saw, that Tom Dold was worried too. I knew that Ellen was hard hit. She had spent thousands trying to solve the mystery of Cousin Albert and Willy, hoping to find their bodies. Some of this had gone to unscrupulous characters who preyed on her. Most of it she had borrowed. Now for some time banks and private lenders had been calling in their notes. Money was hard to get. Ellen was forced to sell thousands of sheep to the packing houses, and the pitifully small price per head was quickly swallowed up in interest and running expenses. I had hoped that Mama Grande's death might leave enough to pay Ellen's debts. I had heard stories of fortunes in gold and silver that Mexican ricos, afraid to trust banks, kept buried under their houses. But if Mama Grande had any secret hoard, we never knew of it. All she left was her share in the ranch, evenly divided between her two surviving daughters, and this brought not a dollar to Ellen.

It was singular to see Ellen unworried. The worse her situation, the more her debtors hounded her, the more it seemed to mend the deep wounds of her unsolved tragedy, to help her believe that perhaps

Willy's and Albert's deaths were for the best after all. Almost never, except late at night, could she be found in her room. She and Critter were inseparable again. She drove him and her yellow-top buggy everywhere, to the ranch to manage what she had left, to her creditors to appease and stave them off, to her old Mexican family friends to borrow a little so she might hold on until better times returned.

It all agreed with her. Activity was her nature. I never saw her looking better. There were no visible signs of debts or difficulty. If anyone looked worried, it was Tom Dold or Mr. Kidd or the doctor or myself. When Mr. Kidd offered me a job at the commission house, I jumped at the chance. It meant I could contribute a little toward our expenses of living, although I knew I never dare mention this to Ellen. As it was, she felt plainly hurt when I told her.

"You're only a boy, Jud. You should be in school."

"I'm fifteen," I told her. "Lots of boys go to work at twelve."

"Is it that you miss Willy? Are you too alone in the house?"

I nodded. She was silent a long time and I knew of what she was thinking.

"Very well. Then I give my consent. But you

must never leave me, Jud. Remember, this house is yours as long as you live."

It was like a breath of fresh air and a new life to leave the gloomy old white casa for the commission house, if only in the daytime. Young as I was, I became a member of the commission-house clan. I found it a big jolly family, free from tragedy, and very much alive, patronizing the same restaurant, dance hall, and livery stable, taking the same train to Trinidad on holidays, playing tricks on one another and especially on me, the newest member. We had a mandolin-and-guitar club, and one evening a week those off duty got together in Mr. Younger's office to practice the latest Eastern songs and pieces.

And yet through all my daily life in this hive of commerce, through the scent of sheep-dip and hides and of horses and mules from the loading platforms; through the sounds of business, banter, and the scratch of ledger pens; through the gray-brown dust of sandstorms and the white dust of unloading flour, I couldn't shut out the ugly day-by-day reports from the panic-ridden range, the sad things that were happening to others and which inevitably must engulf Ellen and the old Johnson y Campo name. The tragic part was that men still had to fight for their existence when times at last had begun to improve. The cycle had turned. Rain was already falling on the range, new grass appearing. Wool and lamb prices had steadied. The worst was over and most ranchers had begun to breathe hopefully again.

That was when Beasley played his hand. All through the months of drought and panic when expenses were heartbreaking and income non-existent or trifling, he let Ellen struggle with Rancho Zelandia. But once the hardest times were over and promise of recovery and profit began to appear, then in the name of his half-owner wife he entered suit, filing a bill in equity, citing mismanagement, neglect, and non-payment of interest and principal on Ellen's notes which he had bought up in his wife's name, demanding an accounting, a receivership, and public sale of the ranch's real and personal property.

He entered the suit swiftly and without warning while court was still in session, and Judge Saxton put it through at the end of the term. Tom Dold struggled manfully, but he was no match for the weight of debt and charges which were true of many ranchers in these days. Moreover, Ellen refused to testify on any allegation that would make out her sister a liar.

"That's Snell, not Ana, speaking," was all she

would say. Even if Judge Saxton had not owed his
appointment to Beasley's influence, he would have
had little choice in the matter. The case was heard
without jury. Beasley's law partner, George Steffy,
was named as receiver and the ranch and stock put
on the block. Few except Ellen dared offend Beasley
by bidding, and Ellen had neither cash nor collat-
eral left to do it, nor wealthy friends to come to her
assistance. The famous old Johnson y Campo ranch
and stock, including the Grant, were bought by
Beasley for less than fifty thousand, none of which
would be divided with Ellen. Her share was to be
paid to her sister on Ellen's unpaid debts.

I heard of the final blow at the commission house
one afternoon. The same day Pas Ramírez, now a
loader, cornered me against a car of outgoing
wool.

"It is too bad, but she will fix him now?" he said.

"I don't know what you mean, Pas," I told him.

"Oh, you know, but you don't like to say it right
out. You think it might be used in court against her.
Don't worry, amigo. I would say nothing."

"I'm still not sure what you mean. If you mean
what I think you do, you are dead wrong."

"No, you are the one who is wrong, amigo," he
told me. "I know she has waited a long time. Years
ago the wolf howled for his due. But the Anglo in

her waited, thinking the foolish Anglo thought that
if you pet him the wolf will turn into a dog. Sometimes the Spanish and Indian also wait a long time.
But they know the wolf will always be a wolf. They
wait for the best time to suit their purpose, and in
the end they move. Now she has no other way. He
has everything and she has nothing. She will not
let him take the ranch, the only thing she has left.
She will fix him now like she fixed Frank Jeffcoat
long ago."

I went home hating to face Ellen that evening,
but she wasn't at the house. The Wilmots had taken
her home to dinner after the sheriff's sale. Chepa
said she had sent word that it would be late when she
came in. During the evening Dr. Gammel called
and I told him where she was. Knowing he would be
with her made me feel a little better. I didn't hear
her when she came, and her door was closed when I
went to the commission house in the morning.

But Chepa and Epifania told me enough. Their
faces were dark and bitter.

"You know, Señor Jud?" they asked. They had
added the "señor" only since I worked at the commission house.

"Yes, I know," I told them gloomily.

"She dare touch nothing on the ranch, only a few
little things that he will say belong to her. Ay de mí!

Did you ever hear of such a thing! What will become of her now?"

"I don't know," I told them, eating breakfast as fast as I could.

"There is a message for you," Chepa said. "She told me last night when she came in. She must go out to the ranch tomorrow. It is the last time. You must go with her."

I winced at that. It was like Ellen. Not, could I get off from work, but I must take off and go along. That day when I asked Mr. Kidd for leave, he gave me a look from under his black eyebrows and ordered me into his office. This was the mysterious, exclusive, unattainable room I had long wanted to see, but I scarcely looked around at it today.

"You know that this is the end of her and the ranch?" he asked.

"I'm afraid it is, sir."

"What is she going to do? How does she expect to live?"

"I don't know, sir."

"I suppose you think I should have given her a hand?"

"I didn't think about it, sir."

"Have you ever looked in our books?"

"Just my own ledger, sir."

"Well, if you had, you'd have found that we car-

ried her for some nineteen thousand dollars. I could
have sold the debt to Beasley long ago at twenty
cents on the dollar. I didn't then, although it looked
at the time like we'd never get a penny. You know
that, don't you?"

"I don't know, sir."

Mr. Kidd looked at me. His eyes and eyebrows
were both very dark. I knew she could expect no
more help from that quarter.

"You don't know? What do you mean?"

"I don't know what I mean, sir."

"I think I know. It's no use, Jud. It's too late."

I had no idea what he meant. He sat for a long
time staring away from me. The only thing in his
line of vision was the painting of a naked and volup-
tuous woman half covered by a rare old Navajo
blanket on the wall. He went on.

"You mean she's always been a lady."

"Yes, sir," I said, but that wasn't exactly what I
meant.

"Jud, do you know what a lady is?"

"Yes, sir. I think I do."

"I don't think you do. A lady is a woman of great
harm or position or both who because of it has
never had to do anything for herself but has always
had somebody to do it for her. Did you ever think of
that before?"

"No, sir."

"Well, it's time you understood some of these things. Ellen was a Johnson y Campo. If there was a Campo who had more than she had, I never heard of it. She was born to the purple, to the ranch, to the family name, and money. There was always something or somebody to take care of her. When she was young, it was her father. When Frank Jeffcoat ruined her garden and one of them shot him, she had her brother Charley to fall back on. When Charley was tried, she had Albert to free him and to convict his murderers when they came to trial for another crime. Now Albert and Charley are gone. Her father and mother are gone. The ranch and her money are gone. She needs someone more than ever, somebody to take up her cause, solve her problems, and take care of her. There she is, attractive, beautiful, worldly. Tom Dold is a gentleman, but he's not your Cousin Albert by a long shot, and George Gammel drinks too much most of the time. There's nobody left to come to her rescue any more."

I kept thinking about it on the way to the ranch next morning with Ellen. The mesa had never looked more beautiful, the air like wine, the Prieta crystal clear, and the ranch headquarters, when w came to it, like the capitol of some small empire. It had rained during the night and the Johnson y

Campo range looked fresh and green. It was the only time I recall that I would have preferred a sandstorm. With the sky gray, the sun a dull red ball, and dust flying, the ranch wouldn't have been so hard to give up.

Today it was an ordeal. I had never seen Fidel's face so grave as when he came to take Critter. Even the Casa Grande looked more desirable now that it was no longer Ellen's.

As we came up on the portal, one of the doors opened and Snell Beasley, thick, active, all business, appeared.

"You can come in," he said curtly, and I looked to see how Ellen liked being invited into her own house. She gave no sign, entering the familiar sala almost as a visitor, seating herself presently in the chair Beasley indicated, as if this house was not part of her, as if she hadn't been born in one room and spent much of her life in the others.

"I had hoped Ana would be here," she said quietly.

"No," Beasley answered. Then as if something in her remark had nettled him, he went on sharply: "Before we get to the few things you may claim, I want to tell you that I might have claimed a good deal more. We could have taken everything you have, the house in town and your horse and buggy."

All she said was a low "Thank you."

"No," he said heavily, "we don't want your house now or your horse. He's getting up in years. I have a better one. Now shall we get down to business?"

All through the scenes that followed I marveled at Ellen. How could she go through in a couple of hours what would normally take days to dispose of? How could she give up all this so calmly? What was going on in her head? Was she really the one she had been acting the role of lately, the gentlewoman courteously agreeing, accepting, taking with good grace her humiliation? Or could she be waiting like Pas implied, letting Beasley do his worst, seeing how far he would go, which would give her final violent act all the more reason and sympathy? Without some planned solution in her mind, I felt she couldn't control herself like this.

In the end she had me carry some small things to the buggy. She asked her brother-in-law to deliver the rest with Teofilo or Fidel.

"Now we must go, Jud," she said.

First she drove around the ranch headquarters, the lambing pens, the chapel, then to the edge of the cedars where Willy and I used to ride. She was taking a last look at everything.

"Look," she said once, "I don't need to touch a line. He knows where to go."

It was true. Critter seemed to know. He went to the cemetery and beyond it to a spot where the whole Grant could be seen spread out before us with the Greenhorn Mountains a white crown to the north.

"I think Critter wants to see it himself," Ellen said. Then to the horse, "Now that's enough. He'll think we're stealing something. Sooner or later we've got to go home."

When we returned to headquarters, the Mexicans, who had been watching, were waiting for us. It was a scene like I had witnessed before but not with today's implications. I saw again that, charming as she could be with her own kind, she was at her best with those below her, with children, servants, peons, those who looked up to her, Mexicans or Anglos. Then something transformed her and she burned with a purity and simplicity that is difficult to set down. No actress could have matched her. She stepped down from the buggy to shake every hand, had a word in Spanish for each, an act that caused many of them, especially older men and women, to break down and fall on their knees, kissing her hand or skirt, pouring out their memories of her father and mother and Don Carlos.

What Beasley must have thought if he watched from the window, I have no idea. But as we drove up through the canyon I bled for her. I began to see more clearly what Mr. Kidd had said, that always she had had this great ranch behind her, someone to espouse her cause and solve her problems. What had she left now? To whom could she go any more? All she had were a house in town, an old horse, and a young stripling like me.

As for Critter, he seemed weary as I. Once we had left the steeper downslope where the buggy rolled of its own volition, I noticed that he dragged. It was true he had already traveled from town to ranch that day, but there had been a time when twenty miles would scarcely have laid a hair on him.

I mentioned something of this to Ellen.

"He's older," she said. "But not old. He's still younger than Willy. They were born almost on the same day two years apart."

Just the way she said it made me glance at her. She sat there on the faded cushions of her yellow-top buggy, erect, well dressed as always, her suit coat and skirt of the best English material, her little green hat with the feather jaunty, her driving gloves open at the wrist and flaring in the genteel manner.

"He's older," I insisted. "We're all older."

"He says you're older, boy," she said.

At the sound, Critter broke at once into a faster

pace, but presently slowed again to his old trot. We were well on the mesa when I glanced back and saw another rig behind us, just emerging from the cedars at the mouth of the canyon. Farther out on the mesa I looked again. It was still there, almost the same distance behind us as before. Whoever it was showed no disposition to close the gap between. But when we reached the pile of rocks blackened on one side from fires of generations of leñeros, I thought the rig was definitely nearer and that the horse looked like Beasley's.

Ellen never looked back at all. We passed the region of rolling lomas, crossed the big cañada and the Prieta Wash, and were on the almost level part of the mesa when I thought I heard a steel shoe strike a stone. Glancing again, I saw the rig closer behind us now and coming fast. It was definitely the runabout and the racer with Beasley himself driving. I'm sure Critter heard the sound, too. His ears had pricked and his pace increased. Ellen heard it now and looked over her shoulder.

Afterward she told Tom and me that her first impulse had been to turn Critter directly off the road to the north. She guessed at once, as did I, that Beasley had chosen the spot to race, that he was unsatisfied with taking the ranch and sheep, that now with the town just ahead of us in plain view across the river he intended to beat her horse and take the only laurels she had left. For a moment, she told us, she hesitated to humiliate Critter, make him show the white feather, and by the time she had made up her mind it was too late. Critter had definitely accepted the challenge.

I had been in races behind Critter before and have been in others since, but there was something about this one that troubled me from the start. Even the mesa, the sight of Moro lying spread out on the river plain below, and the low Tecoletenos Mountains far on the horizon had a different look and feel today. But it was Critter who moved me the most, no longer the pet but the old servitor unwilling to admit his years.

Some men mellow as they age, leave the fires of manhood behind them and handle better than in their youth. Critter was none of these. Ellen knew it, I'm sure. I had seen her half stand at the lines before, but never her shoes so planted on the foot iron, her body weight and strength thrown against the bit. I still don't know, was it her long aversion to race Critter or her woman's intuition to try to save him from his first defeat? Either way, there was no stopping him today more than any other time. This she soon found out. He had the will to go, and there was nothing to do but let him have his way.

I did feel that Critter had the advantage of the road. The racer would have to take the rougher ground beside it. Critter's mane and tail were streaming and yet as we went on something in him fell short. I remembered his old effortlessness, when without the benefit of trying he seemed to fly like the road-runner, half on the ground, half in the air. Today he seemed to run as fast as he ever did, but the magic of easy power was lacking. I could feel the undercurrents of exertion, striving, and strain.

Slowly but steadily the racer pulled up beside him. When he was younger, the near approach of the other horse would have been the signal for Critter to let loose a burst of speed that would have left his rival far behind. Now it was apparent that Critter had already given his best. I had a glimpse of Beasley squatting forward on his light runabout seat, his arms outstretched. As he came abreast he threw us a curious cool, almost impassive look, then flicked his whip and the chestnut started pulling ahead.

"Help me, Jud!" Ellen suddenly panted.

She was having trouble with the right-hand line, I noticed, and the moment I took hold of it with

her, I knew why she had called me. Critter was pulling hard toward his rival. I used both hands but
without effect. Despite our three arms, there was no
holding him. We might as well be pulling on a loco-
motive. Never had he let a horse around him, and
he wouldn't now. I fancied I saw the wild look in his
eye toward his rival. Then with a furious swerve
that carried us with him like matchsticks he threw
himself against the chestnut and all was lost in a
crashing of buggies and bodies and horses upturned
with their legs in the air.

They said afterward that a dozen people in Moro
watched the race, that it was especially visible from
the depot and the commission house, where men
quickly climbed to the roof to see the outcome. In
almost no time riders and rigs were hurrying to ford
the river and reach the scene. What had happened
they couldn't tell from town, but they knew it was
bad. What they found was a boy with a broken arm,
a woman with a scarred and bleeding face, one
horse still on the ground, the other standing quietly
by in broken shafts, his only sign of disaster the
brown dirt smeared on his sweated hide. That was
the racer, but his driver lay under the overturned
runabout, and when strong hands righted it, he
still lay unmoving.

Ellen waited till Dr. Gammel finished with him.

"Look at Critter!" then she begged him, which he did.

"He's done for. The broken shaft hooked him. He looks like he hit barb wire. I doubt if he's got any blood left. The kindest thing you can do for him is let me shoot him and put him out of his misery."

Such a look of blinding anger came into Ellen's eyes that I thought the doctor quailed.

"I would shoot you first, George!" she told him, and sent to town for Manuel.

We stayed until Manuel came and for some time afterward, until Critter was on his unsteady feet. Then we drove down with Tom Dold in his buggy. People on Audiencia Street and the plaza watched silently as we drove by. When we reached La Placita, a little group stood in front of the Beasley house.

"I must go to Ana first," Ellen said.

I followed with my bandaged arm. Tom Dold and the doctor helped her up the steps. She did not knock. One of them opened the door for her and she went in. I had a glimpse of Ana surrounded by Beasley's friends and their wives. What would happen now I had no notion. But when Ana looked up and saw Ellen, it was as if no one but they were in the room. A strange nameless cry rose from each of them, and the two sisters ran into each other's arms.

I watched them for a long moment. Tears flowed
from them both. It was the first time I had seen
Ellen cry. The pair kept embracing, comforting,
chattering to each other, as only the Spanish can.
It was strange that at a time like this I should remember what Mr. Kidd had said, that Ellen's deliv-
erers were all gone, that there was no one left to
rescue a lady any more, and yet here she was, delivered in the arms of her only sister, the widow of
probably the richest man in the territory.

I wish it were possible to add that Willy and
Cousin Albert came back. For years I kept saying
to myself, it can't end like this—they will surely
turn up someday. But they never did. Their bodies
were never found. Only the whispering wind knows
where they lie, for those unknown men involved in
it must be dead today. Now, looking back over sixty
years, I feel this may be the reason why the unsolved mystery remains to many of us the most
haunting of earlier happenings in the annals of
New Mexico.